THE
HUNGRY YEAR

OTHER BOOKS BY
CONNIE BRUMMEL CROOK

NELLIE L.

NELLIE'S QUEST

NELLIE'S VICTORY

FLIGHT

MEYERS' CREEK

LAURA'S CHOICE

MAPLE MOON

LAURA SECORD'S BRAVE WALK

THE
HUNGRY YEAR

CONNIE BRUMMEL CROOK

Thousands came ere hundreds could be fed.
— WILLIAM KIRBY, *CANADIAN IDYLLS*

Stoddart Kids
TORONTO • NEW YORK

Published in Canada in 2001 by
Stoddart Kids, a division of
Stoddart Publishing Co. Limited
895 Don Mills Road, 400-2 Park Centre, Toronto, Ontario M3C 1W3

Published in the United States in 2001 by
Stoddart Kids, a division of
Stoddart Publishing Co. Limited
PMB 128, 4500 Witmer Estates, Niagara Falls, New York 14305-1386

www.stoddartkids.com

To order Stoddart books please contact General Distribution Services
In Canada Tel. (416) 213-1919 Fax (416) 213-1917
Email cservice@genpub.com
In the United States Toll-free tel. 1-800-805-1083 Toll-free fax 1-800-481-6207
Email gdsinc@genpub.com

05 04 03 02   3 4 5 6

National Library of Canada Cataloguing in Publication Data
Crook, Connie Brummel
The hungry year

ISBN 0-7737-6206-X

1. United Empire Loyalists — Juvenile fiction. I. Title.

PS8555.R6113H86 2001   jC813'.54   C00-932981-1
PZ7.C8818Hu 2001

*We acknowledge for their financial support of our publishing program the
Government of Canada through the Book Publishing Industry Development
Program (BPIDP), the Canada Council, and the Ontario Arts Council.*

Printed and bound in Canada

To my talented daughter Debbie,
who fills her roles expertly as teacher, homemaker,
wife, friend to many, and mother of twins,
Alex and Ryan, and their brother, Jordan.

CONTENTS

ACKNOWLEDGEMENTS

I would like to thank Mrs. Katherine A. Staples, manager of the Loyalist Cultural Centre at Adolphustown, Ontario, for sending me files and maps preserved from the times of early settlements in the Adolphustown and Fredericksburgh townships, and for answering so cheerfully my many questions about that time period in Canadian history. I found her knowledge most helpful and her enthusiasm inspiring.

Also, thanks to my nephew Rob Bruce of Belleville, Ontario, who described in detail for me the appearance of bears and wolves sighted on his parents' farm at Madoc. Thanks to my cousins, Thornton and Doris Brummel of Napanee, Ontario for their research and answers to questions about the Napanee and Hay Bay areas where they have lived most of their lives.

A special thanks to Beulah Marie Antone Steele of Peterborough for suggesting the name of Gajijáwi for the Mohawk woman in this story and also to the late Aileen Irons of Curve Lake Reserve for suggesting the names of Tówi and Desagósnye.

A very special thanks to Kathryn Cole of Stoddart Kids for her helpful suggestions.

PART ONE

❖

Into the Forest

CHAPTER
ONE

Kate woke up with a gasp. Was somebody breaking into their wagon? She shifted slightly in her bed, trying not to make a sound. There it was again: a clawing noise just behind her head, on the other side of the canvas curtain that separated the driver's seat from the rest of the wagon. Kate sat bolt upright in fear, then immediately wished she hadn't. Now whoever or whatever was making the noise would know there was someone in the wagon.

Kate sat very still, trying not to breathe too hard. The noise from the driver's seat had stopped. All she could hear now were the waves lapping against the shore of Lake Ontario and scampering sounds coming from the forest on the other side of the wagon. Kate stole a glance at her brothers sleeping in the trundle bed next to hers. Their blankets were pulled right up to their noses to protect them from the cold October air.

Kate stared at the dim light filtering through the canvas covering at the back of the wagon. Father and the Shaws must still be up talking. Kate couldn't help feeling resentful. There was Father having a good time with his friends and here she was left to protect the boys. It had been that way ever since last winter when her grandma died.

If only Father hadn't made them leave their home! They'd left their farm near Albany almost two months before, and had been travelling ever since. Now here they were in Canada, in the year 1787, at the log cabin of Father's friend, Will Shaw, and his family.

The rustling came again from the front of the canvas curtain. Kate shuffled towards the top of her bed and listened. Was someone trying to steal the wagon? No, that was impossible. The horses were tied behind the barn, and no one would try to steal a wagon without horses.

Maybe it was a wolf, or a rabid fox. Kate realized she was trembling and tried to stop herself. She mustn't act like a coward. After all, she was twelve years old, almost a woman! Father would be ashamed of her.

Kate brushed back her thick auburn hair and moved her hand gingerly towards the curtain. But before she could touch it, something big and furry bulged through the crack between the two panels. Kate jumped back to the end of the bed and stifled a scream. Now she knew it was not a thief, but that was small consolation. It couldn't be a bear. It was probably a raccoon. Through the gap, Kate saw two close-set green eyes glowing in the dark. As she stared, the moon moved out from behind a cloud and its light streamed into the wagon. The green eyes stared right back at her and blinked. There was silence for a few seconds, followed by an unearthly meow. Puzzled, Kate drew back the far end of the curtain to get a better look. There in the moonlight she saw the strangest animal. It was grey with black stripes, about the size of a large domestic cat; but its hind legs were high and its tail was short, like a bobcat's. Its stubby ringed tail was twitching back and forth. Obviously the animal was not happy.

He probably belongs to the farm next door, Kate thought. I'll just catch him and take him into the cabin.

Kate held out her hand and waited for the cat — if that's what it really was — to approach her. He sniffed the air, flicked his tail, and licked his right front paw. A few minutes passed before he moved warily towards her.

When he was within reach, she lifted her hand to pet the cat's head. But he sprang back out onto the buckboard, leapt again, and landed halfway up the trunk of a nearby maple tree.

Kate gasped. She had never seen a cat jump that far. The animal scrambled up the tree and walked out onto a branch that stretched in front of the wagon. Still, it kept its eyes rivetted on her.

"You go chase mice," Kate said with a little laugh. "I can't catch you now. I'm going back to sleep." She turned around and crawled onto her bed.

Relief settled over her like a blanket. Kate often wished she were more courageous. She had tried hard to be brave when her mother died giving birth to her brothers four years ago at the end of the Revolution. Then, after Grandma died, and during the long journey north from Albany, she had cooked and cared for her father and brothers, locking away her own fears in order to keep them happy. Yet Father never praised her. There were whole days when he hardly seemed to notice that he had children; and when he did, it was only to scold them.

"Kate!" It was Alex, one of the twins. Kate leaned over and held out her hand to her brother.

"What is it?" she asked.

"I heard a noise. I'm scared." A head of thick, straight blond hair appeared over the edge of the bed. Alex, with his big blue eyes, stared into his sister's deep brown ones. "Can I come up there with you?"

Kate sighed. "You're fine where you are. You have Ryan with you. Now lie down, Alex." She settled back onto her bed and closed her eyes.

Alex would not be put off easily. He jumped up beside Kate. "Ryan's asleep. He won't miss me," he said. He stared back down at his identical twin sleeping peacefully on the trundle bed.

"Oh, all right, then." Kate pointed, "Grab that quilt." She snuggled under her own quilts while Alex pulled up the extra one and wrapped it around his chubby frame.

In a few minutes, Kate could hear Alex's gentle breathing. She looked over at Ryan, who looked so much like Alex that most people couldn't tell them apart. He had not woken up, but that was normal. He always slept more soundly than his brother.

Kate, however, could not get back to sleep. She sat up with her knees tucked under her chin, her nightgown drawn over them and around her ankles, wondering why Father had not come out to check on her and the boys. He was probably telling the Shaws about their journey to Canada and his bad luck at the land office. He had hoped to be on Lake Ontario, either here in the Township of Fredericksburgh or in Adolphustown Township to the west. Many Loyalists had already settled in the area — too many, it turned out. The shore lots along this part of Lake Ontario had all been taken.

Kate remembered arriving at the land office in King's Town, only to be told that, because Father had never enlisted in the King's Service, he did not qualify as a Loyalist. But Father had been prepared and demanded to see Michael Grass, the town's founder and judge. The clerk sent out an errand boy to fetch him while they waited. Kate had had a terrible time trying to keep the boys out of mischief.

"I have a letter from Hans Waltermyer. I believe he's known as John Meyers in these parts," Father finally explained. "He hid in my home many times. He claims I saved his life more than once."

"Let me see the letter." Judge Grass took a few minutes to scan the page.

"Yes, that's John's hand, all right," he said. "I'll see what I can do." Holding the letter, he disappeared into the next room and closed the door.

When he returned, he held an upside-down hat. He sat down at his desk and pushed the hat towards Father. "You may pick a lot number from this hat," he said smiling. "That land will be your portion."

At first, Father refused to take one. "Is my future in the hands of chance?" he asked.

"You're lucky to receive a free lot," Judge Grass answered crisply. "After all, you weren't actively involved with us in the Revolutionary War, and handouts to most Loyalists ended this year." Then he sighed, "But that letter from John Meyers makes you a special case."

"Not actively involved?" Father shot back. "Don't you remember what happened to couriers when the Rebels caught them? People like me — the people who sheltered them — met the same fate: hanged the same day for treason. I call that active involvement."

Judge Grass went a bit red and cleared his throat. "Yes, yes, I know . . . Your service is credited in Meyers' letter. Now *pick* a number." He thrust the hat towards Father, who slowly drew out a slip. Kate didn't like the look on Father's face when he read the paper.

"Well, what'd you get, Mr. O'Carr? Not a swamp, I hope."

Father grimaced and handed the slip to the judge.

"Now that's not so bad. In fact, you're lucky. You won't be far from Hay Bay. It's always best to be near water." Kate didn't like the way the judge talked to Father. "Your lot has been surveyed," Judge Grass continued, "but not cleared, of course. I oversaw much of that survey myself."

"Where exactly is this place?" Father asked.

"A mile north of Hay Bay in Fredericksburgh Township. It won't be hard to find. Just follow the lake and then the bay. When you get to the north shore of

Hay Bay, turn west onto the concession trail. The land's been surveyed and marked with posts. Here's a map. With these directions, you can't go far wrong."

Father took the papers from the judge. "Thank you for your trouble," he said, turning to go out the door. Kate followed, pushing the boys ahead of her.

Now Kate understood Father's disappointment. Here they were, miles from anywhere, going farther into nowhere. And all to end up in a forest so thick you couldn't see through it. This was a far cry from the settled New York State they had just left.

Kate snuggled down into her bed, wishing her father would come soon. They might never get to Hay Bay if some other wild creature came running out of the woods and into the wagon.

"Meow!" It was that cat again.

Kate sat up straight and listened.

"Meowww!" The cry came once more. It sounded as if the poor thing was in trouble.

Kate slipped on her moccasins and grabbed her cloak. She was afraid, but she was *not* going to let that cat suffer.

She jumped off the back of the wagon and headed into the forest in the direction of the sound.

CHAPTER
TWO

At the edge of the forest was a thick growth of cedar, pine, and spruce trees, but there was no sign of the cat. The line between the clearing and the forest shifted between light and darkness as clouds drifted past the moon.

As Kate was turning to go, the cat cried out again — from farther inside the woods. Kate hesitated, then stepped briskly towards the sound. Dogwood and chokecherries blocked her path, but she pushed the branches apart and kept going. Once inside the forest, the treetops hid the moon from sight, though its light still glowed in the sky above her.

It grew darker just as the meow came again — this time from nearby. Kate looked up. The light of the moon had been completely blotted out by the clouds. She pushed through the undergrowth for a while until the moonlight returned. Then she scanned the treetops, hoping to see the cat's silhouette. But she didn't.

I can't rescue the cat if I can't find him, Kate thought. But when she turned to go back to the wagon, she realized she wasn't sure where it was. The undergrowth and trees looked the same on every side. Her heart thumped with panic. She had gone too far! Kate pulled at the rough branches, looking for a path. They weren't heavy, but they whipped her in the arms and face and narrowly missed her eyes. Her heart raced, but she kept going. She had to get out!

Finally, exhausted, she came to a stop. She remembered stories she had heard about people going round and round in circles in the woods and never getting out. Was that what she was doing? How long had she been lost?

Then she heard a sound coming from behind her. It could be a branch falling, she thought. The sound came again. No, it was not a branch. It was more like hands clapping. She turned towards it.

"Help! I'm lost!" Kate shouted.

No response.

"Is there somebody there? Help me get out of here!"

Kate thought she heard muffled words, but the wind was carrying them away. "Clap your hands again," she shouted. "I'm lost!"

This time the sound came more faintly. Kate plunged through the brush again. She wondered why anyone would be clapping their hands in the forest at night, but whoever it was had probably saved her life. She really must have been thrashing her way farther and farther away from the clearing. She kept moving towards the clapping.

When she finally entered the clearing, the moon broke out from behind the clouds, and there in the middle of the stumps and weeds stood her rescuer. It was a young girl about Kate's age, wearing a dark-blue cloak. Her hands were raised above her head, poised to clap again, but when she saw Kate she dropped them and her mouth fell open in shock.

"Who are you? . . . Why . . . I bet you're the girl from the wagon!"

"I'm Kate . . . and . . . I think you saved my life."

"Yes, maybe I did, though I didn't mean to."

"You didn't?"

"Oh! That didn't come out right. I always say the wrong thing. I mean, at first, I thought you were a bear. You were making the *worst* crashing noises. I was clapping to scare you away!"

"Oh." Kate felt ashamed of herself, but the girl just laughed. A lock of carrot-coloured hair fell out the right-hand side of her mobcap.

"Well, I'm glad to meet you, Kate," said the girl. "I'm Sarah Shaw. Your father's having a good chin-wag with my parents. I got so bored with all the talk of war and rough journeys I came outside for a break. Then I heard that poor cat meowing and all that noise in the woods. And speaking of cats — look who's found us!" Kate looked up to where Sarah was pointing, and there in the moonlight, clinging to the lowest branch of a walnut tree, was the strange cat with the long hind legs.

"Hey, Bobcat! Jump down! C'mon, don't be a scaredy-cat." Sarah burst out laughing at her own joke. "Oops," she went on, noticing Kate's silence. "I always laugh at my own jokes. Mother tells me it's unbecoming, but I just can't help it."

The cat walked to the end of the branch and leapt to the ground. Sarah knelt down and gathered the odd-looking cat into the folds of her cape.

"He's *your* cat?" Kate stared at Sarah in envy. Despite the animal's strange, wild looks, he was putting up no resistance and was even purring and nuzzling the pocket hanging out over Sarah's petticoat.

"Yes, he's mine," Sarah sighed as she looked down at the cat. Kate drew her cloak tighter around her body.

"Let's go to the cabin where it's warmer and we can have a good talk," Sarah suggested. "I never meet girls my age . . . and Mother and Grandma would be pleased to meet you."

"Oh, thank you, but I have to get back to the wagon. I can't leave my brothers." Kate knew that Father would just send her back outside to take care of them if she showed up in the cabin.

"Well, why don't we sit and talk in the wagon? I'd like to see inside it anyway. I'm as curious as Bobcat. It's another one of my bad traits."

Kate smiled at her new friend. "Curiosity's not so bad. Come on, we can sit on my bed, and Bobcat can come along, too."

"Bobcat is wonderful," Sarah said, hugging him tight. "And he's a good mouser. Nancy and I both love him."

"Nancy?"

"Oh, she's my sister. She's eight — four years younger than me. We were both so angry when Mother turned him out."

"Turned him out! What for? Did he do something terrible?" Kate stared at the strange animal whose paws were dangling over Sarah's arms. Up close, Kate could see that he had extremely pointed ears. Tufts of hair grew out of them — just like a real bobcat's ears.

"Oh, he didn't do anything bad . . . not really," Sarah said.

"Not really?"

"It's just Ma. She's been fussing so over the new baby."

"Oh. So there's more of you."

"Yes. I have two sisters: Nancy, and Betsy — she's five. And I have two brothers. My older brother, Albert, is fifteen and George, the baby, is only three months old. He was born on the fourth of July, and Mother put Bobcat out of the house the very next week."

Kate put her fingers to her lips to silence Sarah when they reached the wagon. "We'll have to whisper now."

Kate climbed up into the wagon first and gently lifted Alex onto his own bed. Then she hoisted her friend up by the hand. They clambered over Father's bed, then tumbled onto Kate's. Sarah dumped Bobcat onto the quilts, and he sat there purring softly. Kate could hardly believe he was the same animal she had been so afraid of less than an hour before.

"Why did your mother throw Bobcat out of the house?" Kate asked once she and Sarah had placed themselves sideways on the bed and pulled the blanket over them. As Kate talked, she could see her breath.

"No reason, really," Sarah blurted out at full volume. Then, in a whisper, "Oh, I forgot already!" She wrinkled her nose and continued, "Actually, Ma thought Bobcat had tried to smother the baby. He was only sitting on the baby's feet. Could easily have been his head, though, she said — and next time it would be."

"Why would a cat want to sit on a baby's head?"

"They get jealous. That's what Ma says. So they try to smother the baby."

"Really! Well, maybe he could stay in the barn."

"I tried that idea on Ma but she said no. Sometimes Ma takes the baby out there in his basket — when she's helping Pa. The cat's a danger there, too, she says."

"He *is* strange looking," said Kate.

Sarah gave her new friend a cold stare.

"But he has a nice tail," Kate added hastily.

Sarah scratched the cat's ears and smiled. "When I heard him crying I could not bear it, so I sneaked into the kitchen and got this." She dug into her pocket and pulled out a cup with a lid. She opened it and set it down on the blanket beside her. The cat gobbled the food down, upsetting the cup as he licked up the last bit.

"Is he a wildcat?" Kate asked. "Did he just come out of the forest one day?"

"No. He was from our old tabby cat's litter. All the other kittens grew up to be nice tame tabbies like their mother, but this one, he's different." Sarah raised her eyebrows and scrunched up her nose.

"Maybe he took after his father," Kate said. "Do you think he'll let me pet him?"

"Maybe. But he's gone a bit wild. He only lets me touch him because I bring him food every night. Ma doesn't know, but Pa does and he says 'Be careful.' He thinks the cat'll go completely wild one day and join his pa out in the forest, and then I'll never see him again."

Kate reached over to stroke the back of the cat's head. But Bobcat jerked his head around and growled.

"He might get used to you," Sarah said. Then she frowned thoughtfully and asked, "How old are the twins? I heard your pa talking about them."

"Four and a half."

"Uh . . . maybe . . . *you* could take Bobcat. Would you like to?"

Kate shook her head. "I would, but Father would never allow it. He says he has enough to do looking after three children. He gave away my grandma's cat after she died last February."

Sarah looked serious for a moment. "Yes — I heard you lost your ma and then your grandma. That's really sad. So who does the housework?"

"I do. Grandma came right after Mother died and she taught me lots of things."

"Even the washing? I think it's hard enough just helping Ma!" Sarah's voice rose.

"Shhh!" warned Kate. She glanced at the sleeping boys, then back at Sarah. "Washing is the hardest," she agreed. "And with two boys, there's always a lot of mending, too." Sarah's sympathy and obvious admiration warmed Kate. "It doesn't help that we couldn't take much with us when we left."

Sarah looked around the wagon. "Your father said you gave up everything when you left Albany," she said.

"We kept two wagons full of belongings, and four horses. That was all. We sold the horses and most of our goods at Port Oswego before we sailed over to King's Town. Then we bought the basic necessities all over again."

"So you have nothing from back home?"

"Hardly anything." Kate thought about her private box that held a shawl that had been her mother's and a petticoat of her grandmother's. Sometimes when the constant change and frightening unknowns got to be too much, she would take them out and remind herself of home. "It's so strange and frightening here. Albany was much more settled. And our lot is even farther into the forest."

"It *is* pretty much a wilderness up there," Sarah admitted. "And it's late to build a cabin in mid-October. I don't know of anyone who ever went north to settle at *this* time of year. Maybe your pa will change his mind and stay here with someone for the winter."

"I hope so," Kate said. She stared through the canvas at the light coming from the cabin. "Looks like we'll be staying with *you* at the rate Father's going. He's still visiting!"

"I hope he just keeps talking forever!" Sarah blurted out. "Then you could live with us, and I'd be so happy!"

Kate knew that was impossible, but she smiled at her new friend.

"I have to go. Mother will wonder what happened to me!" Sarah gathered up Bobcat's cup and gave him a scratch behind the ears. "You take good care of Kate and the boys, now, Bobcat." Sarah inched her way over the beds and jumped out the back of the wagon. "We'll make more plans in the morning," she said as she turned to go back to the cabin. "Mother'll be expecting you all for breakfast."

Kate was still smiling as she watched Sarah run towards the light, her pockets flapping and her cape flying around her in the wind.

CHAPTER
THREE

"Wake up, wake up!" Alex was yelling into Kate's ears.

"Go back to sleep," Kate mumbled. It did no good. Alex was jumping up and down on Kate's bed. Thump. "Ouch, that's my shoulder!"

"I know. That's to make you get up, lazybones."

"Yeah, time to get up before it's too late!" Ryan shouted.

"Not you, too, Ryan!" Kate groaned. She lifted the quilts just enough to peer out at her brothers. Their thick blond hair was flying up and down and their blue eyes twinkled as they jumped around her, giggling and shouting, "Wake up, Kate!"

"Get down this minute and start dressing," Kate said sternly, trying to sound like a mother. "And do it quietly. I need some more shut-eye." Alex and Ryan jumped off the bed, landed on their trundle, then hit the floor, making the whole wagon bounce.

Kate lay still with her eyes closed for two luxurious minutes. Then she resigned herself to her fate and thrust one leg out from under the covers. She glanced over at her father's bed. The covers were all askew but Father was not there. He must have gone to breakfast already. Why didn't he just stay in the cabin all night, Kate grumbled to herself.

"Now get dressed, boys," she said. They were wrestling each other.

Kate shivered into her long wool stockings and fumbled over her knee garters with cold, stiff fingers. She threw off her nightgown and drew her yellow linen short-gown over the shift that she had left on overnight. Then she tied on her two pockets with a drawstring around her waist and covered them as fast as she could with her two brown petticoats. The outer one was thick and quilted.

"Kate, help me," grunted Alex. He was trying to get his right foot into his breeches, but he had already put his left foot into the right leg. Ryan was sitting on the trundle in his underpants as he tried to put his feet into his woollen stockings.

The boys put on their woollen shirts: Alex a blue one and Ryan a red one. The different colours had been Grandma's way of telling the boys apart.

"I'm coming," Kate said. She gave her skirts a last, annoyed twitch. It seemed the boys would never learn to dress themselves completely. Sometimes she thought they just wanted the attention.

When she had helped them into their knee breeches, she pulled their moccasins out from under the trundle. "Now just slip your feet into these and forget about your boots."

"I like the moccasins best anyway," Ryan smiled up at Kate.

Alex grabbed his and shoved them on his feet. "I beat everybody! I'm all dressed first."

"No, Kate beat everybody!" said Ryan as he slowly pushed his second foot into a moccasin, not even looking up.

Quickly, Kate made up the three beds and pushed the trundle under hers. "C'mon, you two," she said. She jumped out the back of the wagon and turned to wait for the boys. They came rushing forward, trying to knock each other over on the way. Alex reached her first and she lifted him down.

"Let's get some breakfast," Kate said, setting Ryan on the ground. Alex ran on ahead and pounded on the door with both fists while Ryan walked with Kate, holding her hand.

"So is *this* where we're going to live now?" Ryan looked up at his sister solemnly.

"No. Our home's a little farther on."

"Well, we'd better get there pretty soon. That wagon's getting too small." He sighed and hung onto Kate's hand a little tighter.

"It's not far now," Kate said, but she was not sure she was right. The journey from Albany had been a lot longer than she had expected. And the bateau ride had been a nightmare. The water was rough and both the boys had been sick.

Mrs. Shaw stood smiling in the doorway. "Come right in," she said. "Your pa and Alex are already at the table."

She was a plump woman with a pleasant, round face and dimples. Her blond hair was almost all tucked neatly inside her mobcap. She patted Ryan on the head and put her arm around Kate's shoulders as she led the two refugees into the one-room cabin.

Kate was hit instantly by a welcome wall of heat from the fireplace on the other side of the large wooden table. Father and Mr. Shaw, a big red-headed man, were sitting at each end of the table, and Alex had plopped down between two little girls on the far side.

"Hello, Kate," Sarah grinned. She was sitting next to an older woman who looked like a grandmother.

"Squeeze over, children," Mr. Shaw bellowed cheerfully.

"C'mon over here, Kate!" Sarah sprang up and knocked over her porridge. The older woman sitting next to her set it upright and cleaned up the mess, shaking her head. In the light of day, Kate could see that Sarah had grey-green eyes, and freckles that turned into a solid mass when she smiled. Kate sat beside her, placing Ryan between them.

"Now we'll give thanks," said Mr. Shaw. While his eyes circled the table until every head was bowed, Kate caught a glimpse of Sarah's older brother sitting on the right side of his father. Albert had red hair like his father and as many freckles as Sarah. But he had twinkling blue eyes, and he winked at her with one of them. Or did she just imagine it?

After grace, Mrs. Shaw introduced everyone to Kate and Ryan. The older woman was Mr. Shaw's mother.

Then Mrs. Shaw handed Kate and Ryan each a wooden bowl full of oatmeal porridge.

"Where's Bobcat?" Kate whispered to Sarah over Ryan's head.

"Oh, out hunting again, but I put some milk and bread out behind the shed."

On the other side of the table, Alex was enjoying his place between Nancy and Betsy. He looked quite at home. Nancy had dark auburn hair but the same grey-green eyes as Sarah. Little Betsy was smaller than the twins, but she was serving Alex as though she were his mother.

"Lots of budder, please," Alex said. Kate gave him a cold stare. He shouldn't be so greedy, she thought. She looked at her father, but he didn't seem to have noticed.

"Adolphustown — the hamlet that is — is just west of here," Mr. Shaw was saying. "The first settlers took shelter there the first winter. They've since built homes on their own farms out in Adolphustown Township."

"It's a bit confusing with both the hamlet and the township having the same name," said Father.

"I suppose. Well anyway, the hamlet has a general store and a good blacksmith by the name of Casey. By the way, you'll never get time to build a barn for those horses. Why don't I come up with a few men when I've finished building the extra room here for Grandma? We'll help you finish your cabin and afterwards I'll bring back your horses and keep them for you over the winter."

"Thanks." Father looked pleased.

Betsy slapped great chunks of butter on Alex's bread,

then tried to smooth them out by whacking them with a big knife.

"It's all right in chunks," Alex said. "I like it that way."

"Won't you have some of Ma's jam, too?" Betsy asked, licking the knife. Alex nodded and smiled. As she scooped out two heaping globs for Alex's bread, she dripped a line of juice across the bare table.

"So you're going to follow the lake around and then travel along Hay Bay. Your lot's on the north side," Mr. Shaw went on.

"Yes, I know, but . . ." Father started.

"You might find it easier to turn back from here and go north up the Original Road until you get past the east end of the bay. Then just take the concession road on the left to your lot."

"What's the Original Road like?" Father asked.

"Well, it was blazed through a year ago, after Clark's Mill was built in Appanea Falls. But it hasn't been used much. The crops around here have dried up with drought and there's been precious little grain to *be* ground. Anyway, it's a rough trail and there are bears on the uncleared lots."

"Doesn't sound like the kind of route I want to follow with the family. I'll just keep close to the water as I planned. At least then the bears can't come at us from both sides."

"Well, be careful. It's fine along Hay Bay much of the time, but there are some stretches of cliff where it's quite a drop to the water."

"Yep, I'll watch it . . . How many families live in the

two townships?"

Mr. Shaw began to answer Father's question, but Kate stopped listening. It looked like they were going to press on, after all. She looked at Sarah, who had had the same thought. Sarah reached around Ryan and patted Kate's arm in consolation. When breakfast was over, the twins and Betsy went outside to play while Father, Mr. Shaw, and Albert went to the barn to do the chores.

"Sarah and Kate, will you two clear the table and wash the dishes?" Mrs. Shaw said. "Grandma and I have to bathe the baby."

"Yes, Ma, we'd be happy to!" Sarah blurted out, jumping off the bench and knocking over the pitcher of milk.

"Sarah! *Try* to be more careful," Grandma Shaw said with a frown. Then she smiled at her rambunctious granddaughter. "But I am glad you're so enthusiastic about the dishes. We should have visitors like Kate more often."

Sarah grinned at Kate, who smiled back. Kate decided she may as well stop worrying about the future and enjoy herself while she could.

Sarah bounded over to the cupboard and took a linen dish towel off the nail beside it. She threw it at Kate and went outside to get water from the lake. Kate put down the cloth and ran after her. She had no intention of being left in the house to clear the dishes while Sarah had all the fun outside.

In minutes, the two new friends were stumbling back to the cabin, spilling half the water from the bucket they were holding between them.

"Sarah, you forgot to clear the table first. We need space for the baby's bath!"

"Oops, sorry," Sarah said, laughing and tucking away the stray bits of hair that had escaped from under her mobcap. Kate and Sarah gathered up the dishes, stacked them on the counter beside the cupboard, and wiped off the table. There were large streaks of butter and jam at the end where Alex had been sitting.

"Thanks, girls," Mrs. Shaw said, "now you can start in on the dishes."

"You'd think we were in the army," Sarah said under her breath.

Kate smiled and watched as Sarah poured boiling water from the hearth-kettle into a large pan on the side counter. Then she added a little cold water from the bucket at the door. Over at the table, Grandma Shaw was holding the baby boy while Mrs. Shaw set out a pan of warm water and his clean clothes. Kate remembered her own grandma, and she bit her lower lip. She must not show the Shaws how lonely she really was.

"Okay, Ma, now we're ready to roll!" Sarah announced as she added soft soap to the water in the pan, making a low pile of suds. Kate was amazed at how Sarah found something to say about almost everything. When Kate worked, she did so in silence. There was no one to talk to except Father. And Father had not been much fun since Mother had died. He had become even grimmer after the death of Grandma and the loss of the farm.

As Kate looked out the window at the Shaws' stump-filled clearing, all she saw in her mind's eye was the

late-summer sun beaming down on the meadow behind
their two-storey brick home back in New York. She had
been washing dishes that afternoon of August 11, 1787,
when she heard wagon wheels crunching in the front
lane. Quickly she had dried her hands and run to the
front door. Father was there first.

"Back to the kitchen, Kate, and finish those dishes,"
he told her gruffly.

Kate was glad to go. She knew it was the watchman,
come for the third time to collect the taxes that Father
couldn't pay. She didn't want to see Father trying to talk
the watchman into giving him more time.

When Kate got back to the kitchen, Cousin Hezekiah
was there, making himself at home by the table with his
chair tipped back and his pipe in his mouth. He winked
at her

"Better start packing, m'girl," he said.

Kate didn't answer, but went on with the dishes. All
the while, she could hear her father's voice in the front
room, just as she had heard it the previous evening when
Hezekiah had laid out his plan: to pay the taxes and take
the farm off Father's hands. Hezekiah had acted like he
was doing Father a favour until Father had roared, "Give
up my farm? And what do I get in return?"

Hezekiah had turned nasty. "In return, I'll not report
certain Loyalist activities I observed here during the war,
and I'll give you the chance of going up to Canada
instead of to jail!"

Hearing that, Kate had felt sick. She had slept badly,
and in the morning felt even worse. She peeked under

her soap-covered arm at Hezekiah. By the smug look on his face, she guessed that the watchman's visit was no accident. She also guessed that it wouldn't be long before her family joined the rest of the Loyalist families she had seen riding away from their homes with only the belongings they could pack into a covered wagon. But she hadn't expected the moment to come so soon.

Only three days later, on August 14, they were on their way. Father had rushed around in a silent rage during those days, speaking only to bark out orders. Kate never stopped feeling sick with exhaustion, sorrow, and fear.

CHAPTER
FOUR

"What's the matter, Kate? You look pale."

"Oh, it's nothing. I was just remembering."

"Oh." For once, Sarah seemed to have nothing to say. She washed off a plate or two and sighed. "You know, Kate, I get remembering what we went through back home, too. But I just tell myself there's nothing to be done about it now, and thank goodness the British government is taking care of us."

"Taking care of us? I don't call sending Father up to some wilderness 'taking care of us.' It's going to be . . ." Kate did not finish her thought. She didn't want to let on to Sarah how afraid she was. She was frightened to be alone. She was afraid of Father now that he had become such a grumpy tyrant. And she didn't want to admit it, but she was scared of bears.

"Kate, I thought it was going to be horrible, too, but it was an adventure."

"Adventure?"

"Yes, and the government *did* help. They lent us a tent and gave us a cooking kettle. There was one cow between every two families — and spring wheat, peas, corn, and potatoes for seed. Mind you, we didn't come with a group, so we didn't get a cow then. But we have one now."

"You have a cow," said Kate, thinking of the five cows, four horses, twenty pigs, and countless chickens they had had back in Albany. Sarah mistook her dismay for admiration.

"Yep," she said proudly. "She's out in the shed. She's a bit thin and old, but it's better than no cow at all."

"And you lived in a tent with just one cooking kettle?" Maybe it was an adventure for Sarah who had a mother and a father looking after things, but to Kate it sounded like a lot of work.

"Yes, and the things we'd brought from New York, of course," Sarah was saying. "But it got even better. We came too late in '85 to clear the land in time for crops, so we stayed in the tent right through the fall. It was delightful! Pa got the cabin done just in time before the snow started falling. Phew!"

"Sarah, you do like roughing it, I must say," Grandma Shaw interrupted. She must have seen the look on Kate's face. "I prefer living in a cabin, don't you, Kate?"

"Yes, I certainly do — or maybe a nice big house like the one we had on our farm near Albany."

"Now, Kate, we're in a new land. No point in pining about the old days," Grandma Shaw said cheerily as she dressed the baby in a flannel clout and a woollen shirt and handed him back to his mother. "Anyway, things aren't so bad here. We had a good harvest the summer before last, so the winter wasn't bad at all."

"But the fields looked dry as we came along the lake from King's Town," Kate said.

"You're a smart lass, Kate," Mrs. Shaw said. She pulled a long gown over the baby's underclothes. "This past summer, there was a terrible drought in these parts. Hardly any rain from May through August, and all the crops failed. There's many a low cellar this fall."

"But the government will help us, right, Ma?" Sarah smiled.

"Not this year, I'm afraid. They promised help for three years, and this is the fourth." Mrs. Shaw tied the baby's bonnet tightly under his chin and laid him again in Grandma Shaw's arms.

"How will you get through the winter then? I mean, how will *we* get through the winter?" Kate frowned and dried the dish in her hand a little bit harder.

"We'll just have to make do, that's all." Mrs. Shaw's mouth tightened into a hard line as she turned to throw the baby's bathwater out the door. "Will can hunt and fish to add to our food supplies. And anyway, there's no point in worrying. You two just finish up the dishes and then you can show Kate around the place, Sarah. I won't need your help for a little while."

"Hooray!" Sarah yelled, racing to the door to empty the dishwater.

Kate hung up her dish towel. She could not remember the last time she'd had a minute off from doing house-work or caring for . . . "The *boys*!" she shouted.

"What was that, Kate?" Mrs. Shaw said, taking a twig

broom from the corner by the back door.

"The twins! I forgot all about them!"

"Don't worry. They're out in the yard playing with Betsy."

Kate breathed a sigh of relief. She wished they could all stay with the Shaws. It was so much fun having other women around to talk to and share the work. But it was obvious the Shaws had no space.

"Let's go, Kate," Sarah said, whipping off her apron. Once they were safely outside, Sarah whispered, "Let's go out behind the shed and look for Bobcat. He should be coming around for his breakfast pretty soon."

"Ready or not, you must be caught," shouted Betsy, cutting across the yard in front of Sarah and Kate. Ryan and Alex came tearing after her, smelling a bit like the barn, Kate thought. Betsy must have taken them there first.

"Hey, boys," Kate said. "That's not the way you play hide-and-seek! You have to *hide* first!"

"Not the way *we're* playing it!" Alex shot back.

"Oh, all right then, but don't stray out of the yard."

"Don't worry. We're just following *her*!"

Kate turned around in time to see Betsy make a mighty leap into the back of the wagon. Both boys went flying after her, but there was no competition. As they were struggling to climb up the tailgate, she saw Betsy jumping off the driver's seat.

"C'mon, Kate, let's go find Bobcat."

Kate nodded and in a flash the girls had turned around the corner of the house and headed for the far side of the open woodshed.

There they found Bobcat already sunning himself on a high pile of wood. Sarah reached inside her pocket for the piece of dried rabbit she'd been saving for him.

Bobcat leapt down and snatched the morsel right out of Sarah's hand.

"He's hungry," Kate said as she drew out a piece of bread from her pocket. "Will he eat plain bread?"

"He'll eat anything!"

"I wish I had a cat for company," Kate said, kneeling and stroking Bobcat between the ears. "Father doesn't talk to me at all anymore. Sometimes he tells the boys a bedtime story, but usually he's just quiet."

"Maybe he still misses your ma."

"Maybe. I know I do. But the boys don't miss Mother 'cause she died when they were born."

"Were you there when it happened?" asked Sarah curiously.

"I wasn't with Mother, but I was there." Kate looked down to the ground as she thought of that night. "I heard the midwife screaming for Father, and he went into the bedroom. Then everything went quiet . . . and he came out and told me that Mother had gone to heaven. I still don't understand how she could have died so fast. She couldn't even say good-bye."

"I'm sorry."

"Well, Grandma came soon after. She took good care of us." Kate didn't want to talk about how much she missed her mother.

"And we have both a ma and grandma," mused Sarah.

"You know, Kate, you need some help and I know just the right ones for the job."

"Who?"

"Bobcat and me!" Sarah broke into a wide smile. "Mother has lots of help with Grandma and Nancy. I'll go and stay with you until Christmas, and by then we could maybe persuade your father to move back here until spring. You can't clear land or do anything in the winter anyway."

"Sarah! Kate!" It was Mrs. Shaw.

"I wonder what I forgot to do now," Sarah grumbled as they shuffled towards the house.

"Kate!" Now Father was shouting. He sounded annoyed.

"We'd better hurry," Kate said, breaking into a run. Then both girls stopped abruptly, for Kate's whole family was gathered in the wagon. Father was sitting on the driver's seat with a son on each side of him.

"Jump aboard, Kate," Father said as the girls drew up to the wagon. "We're ready to go."

"I won't take a minute to pack my clothes," Sarah said. "And I'll want to take Bobcat, too, Mr. O'Carr. I hope you don't mind."

"What is this all about?" Father frowned at Sarah, but she had already set off for the house.

"Now you wait, young lady," said Mrs. Shaw in a quiet but stern voice. "I need you to help me. You stay right here. You're going nowhere."

"But you have Grandma and Nancy, and Kate doesn't have anyone," protested Sarah.

"That's enough, Sarah. I don't want to hear any more about it."

Kate had already started to climb into the back of the wagon.

Sarah came and stood below her. "I'm sorry, Kate — I thought it was a good idea," she said.

"Me, too." Kate shrugged. "But I knew what Father would say."

Sarah reached up and squeezed Kate's hand.

At the front of the wagon, Father was talking quietly with Mr. Shaw. "Will, I had no idea my daughter was making such plans. Sarah would probably just get home-sick and, as you know, I'd have no time to take her home. The last thing I need is another girl on my hands. Although a *boy* that age could be a real help. I'm sure you understand."

"Yes, I do," Mr. Shaw said. "And Albert and I will be up to help when I finish building Ma's room."

"Thanks, Will . . . we'll be waiting for you. Come on, Kate." Kate let go of Sarah's hand and stumbled through the wagon to the driver's seat. She sat down beside Ryan.

As they drove out of the lane, Kate turned to look back. Sarah was waving her handkerchief wildly in the air and shouting. Kate raised her hand and tried to smile. She tried to shout good-bye, but she couldn't get a word past the hot lump in her throat.

Father tapped the two horses lightly with his switch — first the dapple grey horse and then the bay. The ones they'd had back in New York had been bays. Once when Kate was about six years old, her mother had packed the wagon with raspberries and beans, and they'd driven into Albany to sell them at the General Store. Kate would never forget how the sun glistened on the reddish-brown backs of the horses and how they shook their majestic black manes. Mother had worn her blue-striped linen petticoat and her light-blue short-gown. Her blond curls had lifted in the breeze as they rode along. At the store, they'd picked out a straw bonnet for Kate. After that, her mother had bought her a piece of maple candy from a big jar.

"Kate, mind the twins," Father barked. "They're fidgeting and getting in the way of the reins."

Kate shook herself out of her daydream. Grandma Shaw was right. There was no point in thinking about the old days . . . the days when she had been more than just another burden on Father's hands.

CHAPTER
FIVE

At last Ryan dozed off, and even Alex was still and drowsy. The boys were curled up on the buckboard floor at Kate's feet. Kate sat stiffly beside her father and stared into the forest. Spruce and cedar pressed right into the edge of the trail. This was going to be her future, she thought. Dark and scary and full of bears.

It had been a long day of travelling. They had stopped in Adolphustown only long enough to replace a broken shoe on one of the horses. Kate thought "town" was a complimentary way to describe the blacksmith shop, a very small store, and the shanties that were surrounded by the forest pressing in from all sides.

Since Adolphustown, the way had been unpredictable. In places, the trail was level with the shore. But at other times, like now, the trail was high above the deep, murky water below. Kate shivered as she glanced at the sheer cliff falling down to the waters of Hay Bay. On the opposite side of their path, the forest crowded right up to the edge of the trail. A perfect haven for bears — and if one burst out of the forest . . . Kate closed her eyes. Of course, the horses would head for the cliff.

"Now, Kate, I think we're going to be just fine," Father said. "We'll be past this spot soon, but if the horses are spooked, you grab the nearest boy and jump. I'll be right after you with the other one." Was he reading her thoughts? Kate was too scared to feel grateful. She opened her eyes and stared straight ahead, trying not to look in either direction.

"Aren't we going to stop and camp for the night?" Kate asked. It had been a sunny day, but nightfall was coming earlier now than even a few weeks ago. She knew it would not be safe to travel along this shoreline in the dark.

"Not here, we're not." Even Father sounded tense.

Father kept driving in silence, glancing at the forest and cliff edge. Suddenly the shoreline changed: they came around a bend and the lake extended straight west of them. They had come to a junction with another road.

"We're at the Original Road," Father said. "It goes up to Appanea Falls. We'll travel on it until we reach the first concession road above the bay, and that runs west, just south of our land. We're almost there, Kate!" Even through his tiredness, Kate could hear some enthusiasm in his voice.

The Original Road was not a road at all, but a blazed trail with thick forest that came very close on both sides. Father picked up the musket by his feet and propped it beside him. Kate knew it wasn't primed to shoot. But it could be made ready in less than a minute. She knew, too, that the gunshot would have to hit just the right place to stop a bear!

Kate watched the forest fearfully as Father continued to drive the horses north. Finally he turned the horses west onto an even smaller trail.

"Where are we?" Alex yawned. When no one answered, he opened his eyes wide and started to scream, "I want to go home. Kate, take me home right now." He jumped up from the buckboard, flung himself against her, and wrapped both arms around her knees.

"I can't, Alex. I wish we could go home, but we can't."

Ryan woke up and started to wail, "I'm hungry!" Then he broke into loud crying. Alex looked at his brother and started to cry even louder.

Kate felt so lonely and tired that she could think of nothing to say to comfort the boys.

"Get hold of yourselves, boys," Father said sharply. Then he added in a gentler tone, "We're almost there. Wait! These are the surveyors' marked posts. We've reached our land! See that patch of sunlight coming through the trees? I would guess there's a clearing in this forest."

They left the trail and headed north — straight into the forest. Kate stared ahead in horror. But Father was right. After barely squeezing the horses and wagon through the dense thicket, they arrived at a triangular clearing about two hundred feet across and one hundred feet wide.

"At last!" said Father. "This is where we'll build. We're fortunate there's a clearing like this. It's almost big enough to be a meadow!" His voice was cheerful now.

The boys rubbed the tears from their eyes and stared

at the clearing. It was a quiet spot, for the trees shielded it from the autumn winds. It seemed warmer now, too.

"I have a surprise for you!" Father said, his brown eyes twinkling. "Mrs. Shaw packed us a big box of food. I bet there's all kinds of nice things in there. Maybe even some of the strawberry preserves that you like so much, Alex."

Father's enthusiasm made Kate jump down to the ground.

"Yessir," said Father, lifting the boys out of the wagon, "it's a great spot, don't you think, Kate?"

"Uh . . . yes . . . it's beautiful!"

"Tomorrow we'll start to build our cabin. But right now, I'll get a bonfire going. It'll scare away any wild animals."

Kate looked around her, not knowing what to think about the site for their new home. The clearing was blanketed in goldenrod and purple asters, just like the ones back in New York. But that was the only homey thing about the place. Kate choked back her tears as a blue jay screamed overhead.

◈

Kate woke in the night to a strange, blood-curdling sound. In an instant, she was alert and upright in bed. In the bright light of the moon, she saw her father crouched at the back of the wagon. Fully clothed, he was holding a musket and ready to fire.

Kate heard another shrill howl and this time knew it was the call of a wolf. It was followed by half a dozen howls coming from all sides.

Fear tingled down Kate's back and into her arms and legs. "Father!" The words exploded from her mouth. "Where are they? Are they all around us?"

"No, Kate," Father whispered. "They're in the woods. I can't see a single one. They probably don't even know we're here. Now, go back to sleep. I'll watch." His army cot was still folded against the side of the wagon, as though it had never been put down that night. Kate could see the dark ground outside where the fire had been.

The light of a full moon shone right through the pale canvas roof and lit the whole wagon clearly. Kate looked down at her brothers, breathing quietly in their trundle bed, and then lay back on her feather pillow.

Were they really safe? she wondered. And how many were there? Surely those sounds had not come from the same wolf! She had heard once that wolves ran in packs. Would Father be able to reload his musket fast enough if they all jumped him at once? If only he had shown her how to use a musket.

Suddenly another howl broke through the still night air! She would count the wolves by the howls. She began mumbling, "One . . . two . . . three . . ." Father turned and looked her way but said nothing as another sound came from the woods. "Four . . ." Kate continued.

In the small hours of the morning, the howls finally stopped, and Kate fell into a fitful sleep.

CHAPTER
SIX

The next morning, Kate woke just as the sun was rising. She could hear the crackling of a lively fire nearby and smell the pungent aroma of coffee brewing. She dressed quickly and crawled out the back of the wagon.

Kate hurried over to the warm fire and sat down shivering on a basswood sapling that Father had cut down and set there.

"Good morning, Kate," he said kindly, handing her a hot cup of coffee. "Here, this will warm you."

Kate sipped the coffee. "Where are the wolves?"

"They've gone." Father did not look up at Kate as he stirred the oatmeal porridge in a large iron pot before him. "I doubt they'll be back. I suspect they were just travelling through. Probably they had a drink at Hay Bay and stayed there for the night. They're long gone from here."

"Kate!" It was Alex jumping off the back of the wagon in his nightclothes and running towards them.

"Alex! You'll catch your death of cold. Now, look, you've made your nightshirt wet on the grass." Kate set down her cup, still half full, and carried Alex back to the wagon.

Ryan was waking up, too. "Brrr. It's cold. I'm going to stay in bed."

"That's a good idea, Ryan — at least until I get Alex dressed. It's too cold to stand around and shiver." Kate helped Alex put on his breeches, warm shirts, and moccasins. "You go over and ask Father for porridge. I'll help Ryan."

"I don't want that same porridge!" Alex complained loudly as he sauntered over towards the fire. Father turned, frowning from under his bushy eyebrows. Alex added hastily, "But it *is* warmer over here."

"Good morning, my boy. And how are you this fine day?" Father seemed in a much better mood this morning, Kate thought as she and Ryan followed Alex over to the fire.

"When are we going to have a real house?" Ryan asked in a sad voice.

"Soon. In fact, we'll start work on it today." Father pointed to the trees with the flat of his hand. "With all these trees, I can almost guarantee we'll be sitting in our own house in a couple of weeks."

"Oh, boy!" Alex said. "Will it be just like our house back on the farm?"

"No, I'm afraid not. It'll be much smaller, but it'll do for this winter. Then next winter, we'll use it as a stable for the horses, and we'll have a bigger, better house."

"Will it be strong enough to keep out the wolves?" Kate burst out.

"Wolves!" Alex said. "Are there wolves here, Father?" Both boys had fear in their eyes.

"Little pitchers have big ears, Kate. Remember that," Father mumbled. Then he turned to the boys. "I haven't seen any wolves around. And if I did, I have a musket. You remember how I shot the foxes back home when they tried to steal our sheep?"

Alex nodded and looked relieved. But he set down his wooden bowl of porridge, still half full.

"C'mon, Alex. It's a long time until dinner and you'll be hungry." Kate picked up a spoon to coax him to eat. He smiled and opened his mouth for the big spoonful.

"I think I can see a wolf," Ryan said.

"Where? I don't see any." Kate looked down at her brother, who was staring straight into the fire.

"See? It's a red wolf." He pointed into the flames.

"What a crazy idea, Ryan. Now quit dreaming and eat up your porridge."

While Kate and the boys finished breakfast, Father paced the clearing thoughtfully. He stopped for a long time near a clump of trees almost in the middle of the clearing. Kate washed the breakfast dishes while the boys played tag. Then she joined her father.

"We are going to need more water soon," Kate said. "And anyway, Father, I need to do a big washing."

"Later," said Father. "Right now, I'm starting work on our home."

"Right here?" asked Kate doubtfully.

"See how these four trees almost make a perfect rectangle? I've decided to use them as cornerposts for our cabin. Then I'll dig a big trench along the ground from one tree to the next. I'll fill the trench with logs and bury them down four feet — upright and side by side." Was Father just thinking aloud, or was he really sharing his plans with Kate? She tried hard to imagine what the cabin might look like.

"But the Shaws' cabin had the logs all lying down flat and notched into one another at the corners," she said finally.

"I know that, Kate! But how do you think I could lift the logs up eight feet all by myself?"

"I could help."

"Near the ground, you could. But you'd never be able to help me get the walls high enough. Oh, it could be done if I made skids. But it would take so much more time. No, I like this way the best. I'll just set the logs upright in a trench."

Kate still couldn't quite picture it in her mind's eye. "But how will the logs hold together?"

"They'll support each other. And for extra strength we can use willow roots to tie them together. Like a stockade," said Father. "Of course, we'll caulk the cracks between the logs with clay. We'll need to make our cabin airtight to keep out the cold. Winter will come before long."

"I am beginning to see," said Kate slowly. "But maybe we should wait for Mr. Shaw to come and help."

"I don't want to waste any time getting a solid wall around us," said Father firmly. Kate wondered if he was confident the wolves had gone, after all. "Besides, I don't want to start my new life by being too beholden. I'd like to have the cabin finished when they get here."

Kate nodded her head and looked anxiously at her brothers, who were playing on the other side of the fire. Ryan saw her looking and came running over with Alex on his heels.

"Boys, we're going to start right now to build our new house," Father explained in a gentle voice. "And you are going to help, too." The boys stopped and looked up in surprise. Slowly Father walked straight from one tree to the next, outlining the rectangle. Then he said, "I'm going to dig a trench where I have walked. You can clear away the grass and weeds inside that space. Meanwhile, I have to start felling trees to prepare for logs."

"I can dig a trench," Kate said. "At least, I can get it started while you work on the logs. That way we can get our house faster."

Father looked at Kate as though surprised by her idea. Then he nodded his head. "That would be a real time-saver, Kate."

Kate hoped she had not promised more than she could manage. She had never used a shovel before. As she went to get the shovel from the wagon, she thought about how much Father had been talking and explaining. He'd said more this morning than he had during the whole trip up here.

❖

Two and a half weeks later, in the early afternoon, Kate, her father, and the boys looked at their work. The last

wall was almost finished. They had the wagon backed
right up to the south wall of the cabin where the door
was. So after Father had cut, peeled, and placed a few
more logs, they could just jump out of the wagon and into
the little stockade if any wild animals came. Thankfully
the weather had held, and they had kept warm even
through the cooler nights.

"Father," Kate said. "I *must* wash our clothes. And it's
so bright and sunny today. It's a perfect day for a washing, but I don't have enough water." She had been
bothering Father a lot lately about washing. Her grandmother had trained her well.

"All right, Kate," Father sighed. "I'll go for the
water! I guess I'll still have time to finish that wall later
today. And tomorrow, I'll putty those four panes of glass
into the window before I start making furniture." Father
had carefully packed the glass he had bought at
Adolphustown.

Father laid his axe on the ground and pulled the horses'
collars out from under the front seat of the wagon. "Hey,
boys," he called. "Want to come for a ride?" The boys
came running and jumped into the wagon with a single
bound as Father started to harness the horses.

Kate crawled into the back of the wagon and started
throwing clothes and sheets into an old, round basket. It
seemed that everything was dirty. She hoped she could
find more soft soap. She knew she had packed plenty.

Father walked around the wagon and looked in at
Kate. "I've been thinking. Why don't you just keep those
clothes and your soap in the wagon. You can wash and

rinse everything right in the bay. We'll bring them back here to hang out. Then the two barrels of water we bring back will last us longer."

"But I should use hot water for the washing," Kate said somewhat hesitantly as she thought about it. Father's suggestion would be a lot easier, but still, she hated to think what Grandma would say if she were here.

A slight smile twitched at Father's mouth, "Well, no one will notice if you miss a spot or two, Kate."

It was true. In their solitary clearing in the woods, there was no one around to comment on how clean their shirts were. Kate shrugged. "Well, it'll save a lot of work. It sounds like a good idea to me."

Father looked rather pleased with himself as he walked around to the front of the wagon. Kate joined him on the wagon seat while Alex and Ryan curled up on the floor at their feet.

"Giddyup," Father said as he touched the horses lightly on the backs. They were off for their bumpy ride to the edge of Hay Bay.

"I wish we had a well like we did back home," Kate mumbled.

"We will in due time," Father replied, "but that *is* a two-man job. I couldn't dig deep enough by myself. It takes one man to dig and one to pull up the dirt, pail by pail. But the ground'll be too hard when Will gets here. So that's a job for the spring. And anyway, I'll need to cut and split wood for fuel."

There was just never any end to the things that had to be done, Kate thought. Back home she had taken all this for granted. She wished she was more like her friend Sarah and could think of all this as an adventure.

At the bay, Kate soaped and scrubbed clothes while the boys skipped rocks across the water and Father filled the barrels farther along the shoreline. Some adventure, she thought. Life in Canada was just an endless amount of boring work stretching ahead of her into days and maybe even years.

When they arrived back at the clearing, Father unhitched the horses in silence and gave them a long tether to pasture. He couldn't let them loose when he was felling trees. Then he hurried back to his work.

Kate had thought she would ask Father to set up a clothesline, but as she looked at the dry, warm grass, she decided to lay out all the clothes she had washed. The sun was still quite high in the sky. Everything would dry in no time, and tonight the clean clothes, sheets, and pillow slips would smell of fresh grass and sunshine.

As she spread the pieces around the ground, Alex and Ryan's voices came floating on the light breeze over the clearing. It was a warm, quiet afternoon. When she finished, she lay down on a soft spot in the grass. High in the sky over Kate, a flock of wild geese that was spread out in a V-shape flapped and honked its way southward. Chirping squirrels from the nearby woods scampered about the trees. The boys' voices became more faint as she started to drift off to sleep.

She wasn't sure how long she'd been dozing when she heard her father's loud shout, "Kate! Kate!" She jumped up and looked around her, somewhat startled from waking up so suddenly. "Kate, come take these two over there. I'll be felling this tree soon. They've got to stay out of the way. It's a big one!"

Kate ran across the clearing towards her father. "C'mon, boys," she shouted. "Come and help me." Then she darted through the remaining gap in the wall where the boys were supposed to be playing.

About seventy feet to the west she could hear Father's axe hitting the tree again. His axe hit the sturdy oak with powerful blows. The tree cracked and snapped as it started to fall. "Timber!" Father shouted out.

In that instant, Kate streaked across the clearing towards Alex, who had run closer to the tree and now stood paralyzed looking up at it falling down on him. Father could not see Alex, but he could see Kate running directly in front of the falling tree. "Kate!" he shouted. "Get back!"

But Kate kept on running.

The tree crashed to the ground with a mighty thud. Father ran breathless to the spot but could see nothing of Kate.

"We're over here." Alex's head emerged from just beyond the top end of the tree. He crawled out from between a few thin branches and smiled brightly at his father.

"But Kate . . . where *is* she?" Father asked.

"Here!" Kate pawed her way out from under some branches not far from where Alex had emerged. "I had to throw Alex clear. I was afraid the tree would fall on him."

"Where's Ryan?" Father asked, looking around wildly.

"I'm back here, Father," Ryan said as he poked his head around the cabin. "You told us not to go out there."

Father grabbed Alex by the hand. "Are you all right, son?" he said in a choked voice.

"I'm just fine."

When Father saw he was indeed all right, he said, "How many times have I told you to stay back?"

Alex squirmed and said, "I forgot! Ryan just about caught me. I squeezed through the side of the cabin to get away. I forgot all about the tree when I ran over there."

Kate stood up and brushed off her petticoat. She was shaking and bruised by the fall. She started limping towards the wagon. Then she felt a hand on her shoulder. "Are you all right, Kate?" Father asked.

"Fine," Kate said abruptly.

"That was a brave thing you did," Father said.

Kate just nodded and kept on going to the wagon. But she held her head high and smiled. She felt sore all over, but maybe things would turn out all right in Canada, after all.

CHAPTER
SEVEN

"Hooray! They're here!" Kate shouted as two large Clydesdales and a wagon nosed through the dense growth into the O'Carrs' clearing. She threw down Alex's torn breeches that she had been mending and ran towards the wagon.

Sarah was standing up just behind her father and Albert. Seeing Kate, she jumped out over the side of the slow-moving wagon and right into Kate's arms, almost toppling her friend over.

Will Shaw drew the wagon to a stop while he and Albert stared at the O'Carrs' cabin. The walls and rafters were finished. All it needed was a roof.

"*That's* your cabin?" Mr. Shaw exclaimed.

"Yes, that's it," Father said proudly. "At last, we almost have a home. It looks mighty good to me — and you do, too, Will." He strode right up to the wagon and shook his friend's hand. Then Father nodded at Albert, "I sure appreciate your coming, too."

The two jumped over the side of the wagon. A golden-haired collie followed Albert and sat down right beside him.

Father turned abruptly to Will Shaw, who was still staring at the cabin. "You don't like the looks of it, do you?" Father challenged him, putting his hands on his hips.

"It's not the looks . . . it's those four trees you're using as cornerposts."

"I thought you wouldn't like that. But I tell you, it saved me a pack of time."

"It's a temptation, all right, to build like this. But it's not a good idea," Mr. Shaw said. "When the winds come, it won't stand up to all the blowin'."

"Won't stand up?" Father shouted. "How could it not stand when it's anchored to those four sturdy maples? Have you ever seen the winds around here tear out a tree by its roots?"

"I can't rightly say I have."

"Exactly. Anyway, we're protected in here." This was true. The forest all around them kept back most of the wind. But today the mid-November wind seemed to sweep down from above, rolling crumpled maple and elm leaves along the ground in front of the cabin.

The three men stood together under the bright rays of the morning sun. Father was still admiring his cabin; the other two were silent. The cabin's basswood logs were grey. Kate thought it looked like a ship rising out of a sea of dead, dry leaves. It was about twenty feet square and had a small fieldstone fireplace in the east wall. The stones were stuck together with hardened clay and rose right to the top of the eight-foot wall. Inside, Kate and the boys had placed flat stones to make a hearth. The window and the door faced south towards the forest and, farther along but invisible from the cabin, was Hay Bay.

"Yeah, that cabin is as strong as the trees it's attached to," Father continued. "Four sturdy maples. Who could do better than that?"

"All right, if you insist," Mr. Shaw said doubtfully. "I'd say take it down and start all over again if we had more time, but . . ."

Kate stared at Father and held her breath. After all that time with no home — after the long, gruelling days they had worked on the building! Father looked back at her and smiled. He felt the same way: this was their home and so it would stay.

"We'd better get down to hunting up cedar logs for the roof," Albert said.

Kate turned back to Sarah. "Come, Sarah. I want to show you our woods. There's a wonderful grove of ferns where I've made a place for us to sit and talk." She hoped Father wouldn't spoil her plans, but she knew she would have to ask if there was work to do.

"Father, Sarah and I are going to my playhouse in the woods. And we don't want the boys."

"I can keep the boys here, but fix them some bread and butter first." Kate was overjoyed, but it was short-lived. "And don't stay away long," Father continued. "You know you need to have meals ready for all of us." Kate groaned. It was difficult enough to cook for themselves over an open fire. How was she going to feed these men, too?

"That won't be necessary," said Mr. Shaw. "Jane's

baked enough to feed an army. We plan to share."

"All right," said Father. "But mind, be back before dark."

"I want to go, too," said Ryan, tugging at Kate's petticoat.

Alex marched over to Kate and said, "Yes, we're going with you."

"Well, Kate, they might be in our way here," Father began. Kate's heart sank.

"Hey, Alex and Ryan," Albert said. "Who's going to watch Rover while I'm working? He stays awful close to me and he really needs some company. Come 'ere, Rover." The big collie came loping over from the edge of the forest where he had been sniffing something out. He had four white feet, and the white hair around his neck formed a collar. "Now, Rover, get acquainted with these boys," said Albert. The dog sat down and extended his right paw, first to Alex and then to Ryan. "He'd love it if you threw sticks for him to catch," Albert went on.

"Sure, I'll get a great big stick and throw it right into the forest," said Alex.

"No, let *me* do the first one."

The boys ran around in the clearing, waving sticks in their hands, then throwing them both at once.

"Don't *you* throw, silly," Alex shouted. "He can't chase two at once."

Albert's eyes lingered on the boys for a moment. Only Kate seemed to notice the twinkle in his eyes. He enjoyed watching her brothers playing with his new pet. Then he looked right at Kate and smiled.

Kate gave him a grateful smile back. He was doing it for her, too, she realized. Then she turned to Sarah. "Let's have a picnic," she said, relieved to be free. Sarah nodded and Kate went to get a basket from the covered wagon.

When she returned, Sarah was cutting a small piece of pork from a big chunk. She placed it and a few slices of buttered bread in the bottom of Kate's basket. "This meat's like the army rations," she said. "But they didn't give us any this year. Pa had to buy supplies in King's Town since our harvest was so poor."

"Yes, Father bought some salt pork, too," Kate replied. "And he also got dried peas, potatoes, carrots, and a few pumpkins."

Sarah pulled out a parcel wrapped in cloth and started to unwrap it. "Do you know what this is? Pumpkin-loaf! It's made from pumpkin and cornmeal." She cut off two thick slices, buttered them, and added them to the rations in Kate's basket.

"I thought all your crops dried up last summer," Kate said.

"Not all. Mother, Nancy, and I carried water from the lake for our pumpkins and corn. We must have walked miles and miles altogether. But as the pumpkins grew, their big leaves shaded the ground and held in a bit of moisture for not only the pumpkins but the corn, too. Of course, it was useless to water Pa's crops. But we did have a good number of fair-sized pumpkins, and they'll keep because we cut some up in slices and set them out to dry."

Sarah draped a cloth over the food and pushed the basket's wooden cover on tightly. Then she clasped the handle, and the girls headed out along the western trail.

The sun was shining brightly as they walked between the maple, spruce, and pine trees. Kate had already worn a path to her fern-filled grove. She had even rolled out a few stumps for chairs and made a couch out of old leaves packed tightly together. The boys had helped her trample them into place between split chunks of wood. As there had been no sign of any bears, Father felt it would be safe for them to play there.

"Ah, delightful," said Sarah as she sank down into the leafy couch. "Rapunzel, Rapunzel, let down your hair . . . It's just like a fairy tale here, isn't it?"

"Well, today it is. It's not so much fun when you're not here."

"You could climb that pine tree and be Rapunzel, Kate. And I could be the handsome prince."

"Oh, really? Why don't you be Rapunzel? I don't think I could get up that tree with all these petticoats on."

"Me neither. That's why I was hoping you'd do the Rapunzel part. But on second thought, I don't think you could be the prince either."

"No, but *Albert* would make a handsome prince. Don't you think he's handsome?"

"No!" spluttered Sarah. "He's my brother and has those horrible freckles — just like me!"

They both giggled. Then they were silent. Over the last four weeks Kate had thought of Sarah every day, having imaginary conversations on every subject with her friend. But now that Sarah was actually here, Kate felt shy and strange. Sarah seemed to feel it, too.

"How's Bobcat?" Kate asked finally.

"Poor Bobcat . . . he hasn't shown up the last few days. Pa thinks he's really gone wild this time, but I think he's jealous of the new dog."

"Where did Albert find the dog?"

"Friends in Adolphustown gave the dog to him shortly after you visited us. He's almost full grown, and Albert has been teaching him all kinds of things. I guess he loves Rover as much as I love Bobcat."

"Can the cat survive out in the bush on his own?"

"Pa thinks so. One day last week I found him eating a rabbit behind the woodshed. He must have caught it himself."

"I hope he'll be all right."

"I think so. He's a smart one . . . Speaking of food, let's have a snack."

The girls pried open the picnic basket and reached for the pumpkin-loaf slices. When they had finished eating, they replaced the basket's wooden cover and put a heavy stone on top.

"There, that'll keep the raccoons out," Kate said with satisfaction. "I'm learning lots about surviving in the forest . . . Now, would you like to see the bay?"

"Oh, yes! But do you know the way?"

"Yes, I do," Kate said proudly, brushing off the front of her quilted petticoat. "First you go west along a trail that Father made. Then you go south. It would be closer to go south straight from our cabin, but the forest is too dense."

The girls ran along the western path, kicking up maple leaves as they went. Kate was surprised at how warm it was for mid-November. Before long, they had stepped out into a clearing and were looking south towards Hay Bay.

"Is this still your land?" Sarah asked.

"I think we're a little west of our lot now."

The girls walked south towards the bay. They came to a stop at a cliff that fell sharply to the water's edge. From there, they could see the land across the bay and two farmhouses a mile or so apart.

"Look, you have neighbours!" Sarah smiled.

"Some neighbours. They're so far away. I don't suppose we'll ever get to see them," Kate said.

"Why not? Maybe the bay will freeze over in the winter. It's too bad I don't live over there. As it is, the snow will be too deep in the woods for winter visiting."

They walked a little farther. "Look, Sarah," Kate said. "A campsite!" There was a hole in the ground, the bottom blackened and scorched. A circle had been dug in the hillside around it, forming a natural bench.

"It's probably an Indian campfire," Sarah said as the girls sat down. "This is where the Missisaugas used to live."

Kate leapt up, staring down at Sarah, who looked at her in surprise.

"What's wrong?" Sarah asked.

"Indians! Back in Albany there were horrible tales about scalpings and such. During the war I knew a family who were slaughtered by the Mohawks. They had just moved from near Albany to Cherry Valley."

"I know about the Cherry Valley Massacre," Sarah said calmly. "But it wasn't Mohawks who did the killing. It was a British captain, and he did it without orders. So he blamed it on the Mohawks."

"Are you sure?" asked Kate doubtfully. She sat down again.

"Of course. My parents talked about it for weeks," said Sarah. "You've no reason to fear any Indians around here."

Kate shivered. All this talk of Indians made her nervous. "We should start back," she said.

The return walk to the fern grove seemed longer than the walk out to the bay had been. The shadows were deeper, and Kate wondered how late it was. As they neared the fern grove, Kate broke into a run. She had almost burst into the little clearing when she stopped, frozen.

"What is it?" asked Sarah, bumping right into Kate.

"Get back, Sarah. Look!"

There on the pathway in front of them was a huge mound of black fur. The bear's long claws were shredding the food basket and nosing its contents.

Speechless with terror, Kate and Sarah turned around and ran back the way they had come.

CHAPTER
EIGHT

Hand in hand, the girls ran until they were breathless. Finally, Kate came to a stop, pulling Sarah to a halt with her. They looked back. There was no sign of the bear. But they were too frightened to stay where they were for long. After a quick breath, they were off again — going even farther from the cabin.

They ran west through the maple grove and came close to the edge of the forest. They stopped and looked back again. Still no sign of the big black bear. But there was no welcoming light from the clearing ahead, for darkness had set in swiftly.

"Whatever shall we do?" Kate asked.

"You're asking *me*?"

"We can't go back along that path or we'll just run into the bear."

"The other way's dense forest," said Sarah. "We'd get lost!"

"Maybe we could yell and Father would hear us."

"Where there's one bear, there might be more. They could reach us before our fathers." Just then they heard rustling and crackling sounds in the underbrush. "What's that?" whispered Sarah.

Kate stood still, straining to hear. "Footsteps?" she said.

"Climb a tree!" Sarah yelled.

"That's no help! Black bears can climb!" Kate shouted back, close to tears.

"I don't care! Climb anyway!" Sarah dashed for the lowest hanging limb of a nearby tree.

Kate followed but only managed to make it a small distance up the trunk before she slipped back down. "I can't do it," she said with a catch in her voice that sounded like a sob.

"Yes, you can. Here, take my hand," Sarah said, leaning down from her perch.

Kate took the hand and scrambled up. She was taller than Sarah but much lighter.

They listened again. The noise was coming closer.

"We'd better go up higher," Sarah whispered. She fingered a hold on the trunk, swung herself around to the other side, and climbed up to a higher limb. "I don't think this branch will hold both of us," she said, looking down at Kate. "So I'm going across to that one. As soon as I do, you come up here."

"I can't."

"Why not? It's much nearer than the first branch."

"But you helped me."

"I can tell you're going to be able to climb trees just fine. But first, I'm taking off a petticoat. It's catching on the bark." Sarah threw her thick outer petticoat towards a branch on the other side, but it missed and plopped down onto the pile of leaves below. Her under-petticoat was made of deerskin and could withstand the rough bark.

"I hope I can reach that higher branch when I get up there," Kate said with a sigh.

Sarah skillfully tested her hold and flipped herself around the trunk to a branch on the other side. "It'll be easier if you take off your petticoats, too," Sarah said.

They both knew how cold the nights were getting and that they might be up that tree for a long time. Kate had already thrown one of her petticoats up to a branch above. Luckily it had landed and caught. She was stripping the other linen one when they heard a soft tread just below them.

Without looking, Kate threw the second petticoat. This one also caught and dangled on the very end of the branch. Then, with a pounding heart, she reached for the higher limb and swung her body up onto it. From her position on the branch, Kate looked down and saw a dark figure beneath the tree.

It was the bear.

Kate wrapped her arms and legs around the branch and clung to it, shaking. The only clothes she had on now were her shift, her short-gown, and two dangling pockets fastened to her waist.

Was she shaking with fear or cold? She couldn't be sure. But she did know that in minutes she and Sarah could both be mangled to bits of flesh.

Kate made herself face the bear. It was huge. In her

fear, she thought it looked almost as large as the bull they had had in Albany. And it stank. It was a stifling, musty smell that made Kate cough.

Fortunately, the bear had not noticed. It was busy nuzzling the petticoat Sarah had dropped on the ground. Would it be angry when it discovered the petticoat wasn't food? Next it poked its nose up towards the branch where Sarah lay. Kate gasped as she stared at the giant face and the cold, beady eyes looking up at her friend.

The bear must have heard her gasp, for it swung its nose towards her. Kate stared back and clung to the branch as hard as she could, not even feeling the bark that dug into her arms and legs.

Paralyzed by fear, she looked at the bear's long jaw-line. Its teeth looked as big as an eagle's talons. And the paws half-hidden under those leaves probably hid claws the size of a stump puller.

Kate started to shake violently. Her grip was loosening, and she could do nothing about it, try as she might.

Just then she heard a low growl in the distance.

Kate looked in the direction of the sound and saw a small animal running down the path towards them. It stopped a short distance away and barked loudly.

Rover! Could it really be Albert's dog? That would mean the men were out hunting for them. Kate felt a slight surge of hope, and her shaking stopped.

The bear had turned its head right around and was looking in the direction of the noise.

In the darkness, Kate could just make out the figure of

someone standing beside the dog, holding onto the long hair at the back of its neck.

All was silent as Kate, Sarah, the boy, and his dog waited motionless for the bear to make its next move.

In the stillness, the bear turned and looked at the tree, then the path. After what seemed like a century, it turned and ambled through the underbrush to the south and headed towards Hay Bay.

They all stayed where they were — Kate on her branch, Sarah on hers, and the dog and the boy in the pathway. Kate felt like they had become statues.

Then the boy and the dog came over to the tree, and now Kate could clearly see it was Albert and Rover. Albert leaned his musket and powder horn against the tree trunk and said, "Come down, now. Be careful."

Kate tested each foothold as she descended, then slid down the last stretch of trunk, scratching her arms and legs badly. Albert caught her as she slid. Otherwise, she would have fallen right to the ground.

Sarah scrambled across to Kate's empty branch and, with the help of Albert, made it down to the ground without injury. She slipped into her petticoat.

Kate shook with the cold until Albert handed her both her petticoats. She hadn't noticed him climb up the tree to get them. She had even forgotten she didn't have them on.

Kate slipped on her petticoats while Albert scanned the whole area and picked up his musket and powder horn.

"Lead, Rover," Albert said.

Rover hesitated and looked long at the trail where the bear had disappeared.

"*Lead*," Albert repeated. This time Rover started along the trail ahead of them, but he was still sniffing from side to side with his long, thin nose.

"Hurry now," Albert said to the girls.

Side by side, the girls walked behind Rover. Albert followed close on their heels.

With his musket over one shoulder and his powder horn over the other, Albert looked back along the trail continually until the girls got back to the cabin.

"So there you two are!" Father said as the shaken girls appeared. "Will and I were getting ready to go hunting for you. I told you to be home before dark."

"We would have been except for the bear," Kate blurted out.

"A bear?" said Father. "Are you sure?"

"It *was* a bear, Pa!" said Sarah. Albert and Rover came up behind the girls.

"I thought all the bears would be holed up for the winter!" Father said. He looked amazed.

Kate was shocked. She thought her father knew everything about life in the bush. But he obviously didn't know much about bears.

"It was a bear," said Albert sharply. Then he and Rover turned from the others and disappeared around the side of the Shaws' wagon.

"Albert!" shouted Kate. "You and Rover saved us!"

Sarah started to run around the wagon to fetch her brother back.

Mr. Shaw spoke up firmly, "Let him be, Sarah. Your brother may be a little shaken up, too. He won't want you girls to see that."

A strange silence followed.

Mr. Shaw motioned Sarah to go inside their wagon. Sarah obeyed, but first she ran over to Kate and gave her a big hug.

Kate slowly walked over to her family's wagon and looked inside. The twins were asleep. She stood watching as Father and Mr. Shaw started to build a fire. They probably thought another bear might come out of the forest.

Kate climbed up the wooden ladder that Father had built to help the boys get into the wagon more easily. Her muscles were aching, but she undressed as quickly as she could, put on her nightclothes, and dived under the quilts.

When she closed her eyes, all she could see were claws and foaming bear jaws. After about ten minutes of tossing and turning, she felt even worse. She pulled one quilt off the top of her bed and, wrapping it around herself, walked to the back of the wagon and sat on her father's cot. Through the canvas flaps she could barely make out the figures of her father and Mr. Shaw. They were talking in low tones, but their voices carried in the clear, cold air right over to where Kate was sitting.

"I still think you're making a mistake, David. We should start over. I could go back and get a crew to come up here for a week and rebuild this cabin from scratch. You shouldn't have attached it to those trees."

"No, Will. I made my decision this morning. It'll only take us a few more days to finish the roof, dig the cellar, and put in a floor. I'll be glad for your help with these jobs. Then I can carry on and finish the fireplace and work on the inside myself."

"But you still have to cut wood to burn this winter."

"I'll manage. It isn't as though I haven't cut wood before. But can you still take the horses back with you?"

"Yes, I can. And I see you're determined about the cabin. We'll at least stay and move you inside. Winter could set in any day now."

"That's just the reason I want to move forward."

The men lapsed into silence. But in the firelight, Kate could see that Mr. Shaw was still staring at the cabin.

Kate was shivering inside the quilt as she stared out into the dark woods beyond. Small white flecks floated before her eyes. At first she took no notice of them. Then she realized what they were.

It was snowing!

PART TWO

◈

Trapped!

CHAPTER
NINE

Kate tiptoed to the window and stared out through the one tiny pane of glass that she had scratched free of frost. About fifty feet to the south, she could see huge drifts of snow dappled by moonlight. Just behind them was a wall of spruce, pine, and basswood trees. It seemed as if it had been snowing forever. In reality, it had been snowing for three and a half months — ever since that day in mid-November when Kate and Sarah had met up with the bear.

Today was the last Wednesday in February, and Father had not returned from his day's hunt. Sometimes it took him from sunrise to dusk to hunt down just a few squirrels or a rabbit. So many animals had perished from cold and starvation. The drought of the previous summer had killed off a lot of the wild grasses and crops, and now the snow covered the little forage that was left.

Kate turned around to check the boys. By the light of the candle flickering on the rough-hewn table, she could see their peaceful faces. Under all their quilts, and with the fire that Kate kept well stoked with pine and maple logs, they would be warm. Father had worked long days at the end of November and through December to stock the woodpile.

Kate shivered in her white flannel shift — partly because of the window draft and partly out of fear. Father had never come back this late from the hunt. She looked at the table clock they had brought from Albany that was now on the fireplace mantel. It read half past eight. Maybe Father was on the trail of a buck or a doe. It would be good to fill the empty space in the cold cellar under the cabin. But what could he see out there in the dark?

Kate peered at the cold, moonlit snowdrifts. Were those small slits of shining light the eyes of wild creatures? Was a wolf staring back at her? Maybe a whole pack was about to come racing out of the woods to surround the cabin. And if a bear came out of the forest, it might be able to break down the door. Kate shuddered as she remembered the sharp teeth of the huge creature that had nearly attacked her and Sarah. All was still, however, and not even a small animal scampered over the snow.

"Whoo! Whoo! Whoo!"

Kate jumped at the sound. Up on a maple branch hanging just above the window, she thought she could see an owl staring down.

She felt a sharp jab in her leg. It was Alex, poking her. "I'm hungry," he said.

Kate turned from the window with a sigh and looked at her brother. She knew she should not give him

anything yet. She was rationing out their dwindling
supply of food until Father could find more. Not long
before they went to bed, Kate had given the twins their
supper of bread and cheese. That should have been
enough to take them through the night. She was hungry,
too — and her portions had been even smaller. But she
could not refuse the pleading blue eyes that looked so
much like Mother's.

"I'll see what's in the cupboard," she said, taking Alex
by the hand. She took a partial loaf of bread and cut a
thick slice. In a few days there would be none left, for she
had only a little wheat to crush into flour. Kate pulled
out a wooden bowl and scraped some butter from the
bottom.

"Lots of budder!" Alex directed as he jumped up on
the chair beside his sister.

Kate smiled as she tried to spread the hard butter on
the bread. Then she handed the slice to Alex, who
grasped it with his little hand.

Just then, a thump sounded outside their door. Alex
jumped, and his prized slice of bread fell to the floor.

"What's that, Kate?" he said in a trembling voice.

Kate felt as frightened as Alex looked, but she could
not show it. "Shhh," she warned. She just stared at the
front door and listened.

Silence followed.

Kate began to imagine that a Mohawk man was standing on the stoop, getting ready to scalp them all. Yes,
that's who it probably was, she convinced herself.

Alex scooped his bread off the plank floor, ran for the

trundle bed, and dived under the patchwork quilts beside his sleeping brother. Kate looked towards the window but could see nothing in the deepening darkness.

Then a lighter sound came at the door. It sounded almost like tapping. Was it Father? Why wasn't he calling for Kate to open the door?

Kate crept silently over to the fireplace, hopped up onto Father's captain's chair — a big wood and leather armchair with soft feather cushions — and reached for the loaded musket. Aiming it at the door and taking a deep breath, she spoke out in a steady voice, "Who's there?"

The silence that followed hung heavy in the small cabin.

A tousled head of blond hair emerged from under the quilts. "Shoot it, Kate!" Alex yelled.

"Be *quiet*, Alex," Kate whispered.

"Meow!" yowled the creature at the door.

Meow? Kate frowned and relaxed her hold on the musket.

"Meow! Meow!" The sound came again, much louder this time.

"It's a kitty!" said Alex. Like a streak of lightning, he jumped out of bed and shot across the floor to the door.

"Wait!" shouted Kate. "It may just be a trick." But she was too late. Alex had pulled back the bolt and flung open the door.

There stood the most scraggly looking grey-striped cat that Kate had ever seen. In spite of the cold wind at his back, the animal strolled slowly into the room. His back legs were much longer than his front ones, and he walked with a strange swagger to the left.

"Bobcat?" Kate gasped with surprise. She ran to take a quick look outside. No one was trying to get in behind the cat. She slammed the door shut against the drifting snow.

Alex squatted down in front of the shivering cat.

"Can you shake a paw, like Rover?"

The cat raised its front paw and gave Alex a whack on the wrist.

"Ouch! Bad cat!" Alex backed away.

"You shouldn't have let him in," Kate scolded.

"But it's Bobcat!"

"I'm not so sure," Kate answered. The animal looked awfully bedraggled.

The wind was rising and heavy branches started to hit the house. A blinding gust of snow flashed in front of the window.

"Oh, *please* don't put him out in the storm, Kate," Alex begged. The strange cat, now standing back near the door, was staring hard at both of them.

"Well, he'd better behave himself," Kate said sternly.

"Oh, good! That means he can stay!"

"Quiet, Alex! You'll wake up Ryan. Now go back to bed like a good boy."

Kate swept her brother into her arms and tickled him a little as she carried him giggling over to the bed. She tucked him under the quilts beside Ryan, then leaned over and gave him a kiss on the forehead.

Kate sat down by the fireplace. "Now, Bobcat, is it

really you?" Kate patted her lap. "Come here and let me take a closer look." But the cat had no intention of going to Kate. Instead, he took a fast jump onto the table, then a mighty leap onto a beam that ran across the top of the cabin. From his safe perch, he stared down at Kate.

She stared back. His short tail was grey with black bands and a black tip. It was Bobcat. She was certain of it. The cat flopped his tail over the edge of the beam and blinked his eyes at Kate.

"Well, I guess there's no getting rid of you, Bobcat," Kate said. "I can't imagine how you found us."

Restless, Kate went back to the window. It was snowing even more heavily, and the wind was blowing new drifts around the house. What if Father couldn't find his way home? Kate had an idea. She pushed the table over to the window and centred the candle on the far side so it would shed light outside the cabin for Father.

There was nothing more she could do, so she might as well go to bed. Not often did she and her brothers go to sleep without Father at home. But she was so tired and knew she could not possibly stay awake all night.

Kate slid under her covers, shivering. She stared up at the wooden beam where Bobcat was perched. He swished his tail and looked away.

"Well, it wasn't my idea for you to come all the way out here," Kate said nastily. "You're a lucky cat! I tried to save you back at the Shaws', and now we've saved you from freezing!"

Kate watched until the cat finally curled himself into a more comfortable position and his eyes started to blink shut. She smiled. In spite of what she had just said, it would be nice to have him here. It was so lonely without friends or pets.

Kate pulled her quilt closer around her chin. Her feet were freezing. It would be a long time before she warmed up enough to sleep. To keep herself from worrying, she played a game with herself. She imagined that she was sitting in the fern grove with Sarah, talking about the winter they had just passed through. It was a warm day at the end of May and robins and song sparrows were singing at the top of their lungs.

"Well, about mid-January the winds were blowing so strong," Sarah said in Kate's imagination, "that there was a big draft blowing in under the door. Mother was so busy trying to make the food last longer that she hardly had time to take care of the baby. So I got the job of rocking the cradle. But I was trying to knit a pair of mittens for a friend of mine, and I needed my hands for that."

"So what did you do?"

"Well, I pulled the cradle right over to the door and pushed away the mat that Mother had packed against the crack. The wind rocked the cradle back and forth."

"No. I don't believe it."

"It's true. And it gave me time to finish the second mitt. Right after that, though, Ma caught me and had a fit. 'The baby will die of pneumonia if you keep doing that, Sarah! You're old enough to know better!' Have you ever noticed how parents decide whether you're too old or too young, depending on what they want?"

"Not really. My father scolds me all the time anyway, no matter what I do."

"Fortunately, Mother hadn't noticed what I was doing off and on for those two days. She and Pa were really going crazy trying to cope with the snow and cold. The lake was frozen solid so all the fish had left it for deeper running waters. Anyway, I finished the mitts and they're for you. You'll have them for next winter."

"Oh, Sarah, they're beautiful," Kate would say as she gazed at the bright-red mitts.

Kate's feet were still cold. She closed her eyes and tried to imagine a nice conversation with Father this time.

She could not think of anything interesting to imagine. She found her mind drifting to that day the first week in January when Father discovered the food supplies were getting low. He'd climbed down into the cellar, candle in hand, and gazed around with alarm.

"Kate! Kate!" he yelled. "How could you have let the supplies get down so low! I had no idea. You'll have to feed us less."

"But, Father, I told you . . ." Kate began as he came up the ladder. "I did . . ."

It was true, she had told him earlier in the week, but he had not listened. And he wasn't listening now either. Sitting at the table with his head in his hands, he groaned softly, "How on earth is a man to manage out here in the wilderness with *three children*?"

Father made a trip to Adolphustown to pick up more supplies. He returned in two days, angry and alarmed that he could buy so little. He did not try to hide his feelings from Kate. "The drought last summer left all Loyalists' cellars low," he said. "Some folks are already dipping into next year's seed. King's Town is worse off, they say. A few soldiers from Fort Frontenac set out overland to Montreal after the harbour froze up to get supplies, but a storm came up and they haven't been heard from since. Everyone thinks they've perished."

"Maybe the soldiers will get through," Kate said quietly. She looked at her two chubby brothers jumping over a little wooden horse their father had carved for them out of a piece of basswood. It had been their Christmas present. Father hadn't given her anything. She knew he was just too busy — especially since the boys' horse had taken such a long time out of his wood-cutting schedule.

"I hope so," Father said. "But it's unlikely. My best bet is to head north and hunt for game!"

Kate came back to reality with a jolt. Her bed seemed to be moving. Was that possible? Maybe she was sick from not having enough to eat. Kate rolled over and sat up. She was not sick, but the bed was moving back and forth in a slow rocking motion. The boys' bed was rocking, too, but fortunately they had not woken up.

She looked around the room and saw that all four cabin walls were shaking from the floor up. The cabin's cornerposts — the four sturdy trees — were swaying in the wind.

"Meow!" howled Bobcat, jumping from his beam and landing with a thump on Kate's shins.

As she reached to move Bobcat off her legs, she saw

a flash of light by the window. What could *that* be? Lightning?

No, not lightning, Kate realized to her horror. It was fire!

Flames were licking at the curtains and dancing in front of the window!

Kate sprang from the bed, dragging her top quilt with her. She whipped the curtains with it and they fell to the floor in a flaming heap. She threw the quilt over them to smother the fire completely. But in seconds, a small flame burst through the middle of the quilt and smoke began to billow out from underneath it.

Kate grabbed a corner of the smouldering mass and pulled it towards the door. As Kate flung the door open, a gust of wind and snow blew inside. She stepped out onto the low stoop, yanking the flaming curtains behind her. She hurled them towards a snowbank, and the wind fanned it into full flame before another gust blew a huge pile of snow on the blaze.

Kate stood knee-deep in the snow, grateful for it, for once. She stepped over to the drift and tried to dig out her quilt, but all she found were a few charred pieces and some puffs of smoke. She turned, shaking with cold, and hurried back to the cabin.

Alex was standing in the doorway in his flannel night-shirt, peering at her with huge eyes. "Get back into bed where it's warm, Alex," Kate gasped, jumping onto the stoop. The wind tore at her white mobcap and lashed her hair into frozen clumps against the back of her shift.

Snow had already drifted inside, and she tramped through it, not even trying to kick it back out. She struggled to close the door against a fresh gale of snow and wind. It wasn't easy: the cabin was still rocking and swaying.

Kate knew she would have to get warm quickly. Her shift had been torn and her feet were blue. She shook uncontrollably as she staggered over to the fireplace and held her hands to the warmth.

"Here, Kate," Alex said. Her little brother had dragged over the twins' thick quilt and, with both arms extended, he held it up to her.

Kate was silent as she pulled off the wet, half-frozen shift and wrapped herself in the quilt. It was still warm from her brothers' sleeping bodies. She sank weakly into Father's captain's chair.

"Kate?" Ryan yawned from his spot in the trundle bed. He was rubbing his eyes as he woke up. "What's wrong?"

"Go . . . back . . . to sleep," Kate said, her teeth chattering so hard she could barely speak. "You, too, Alex."

For once, they listened to her. Solemnly, Alex climbed into bed. "Settle down, Ryan," he said importantly. "There was a fire, but Kate and me put it out!"

Kate fetched her clothes from her bed and put everything on, including her shoes. Then she pulled the top quilt off Father's bed and threw it over the boys. She was glad that they had already nodded off. Wrapping herself in their quilt, still a little damp from the snow, she sat down in her father's chair and gazed into the fire.

The flames that had been so frightening before were now starting to soothe her. As the wind died down and the cabin fell into silence, Kate's head dropped to her chest and her eyes closed.

CHAPTER
TEN

Thump . . . Thump . . . Thump . . .

Kate jerked upright. Someone was pounding on the front door. The grey light of early dawn filtered through the window into the little cabin.

"Kate! It's me. Open up!"

"Father!" Kate shouted as she ran to the door and pulled back the bolt. Father stumbled into the room, not even trying to shake the snow from his coat. The hair that fell out from under his heavy fur hat was stiff, and his bushy eyebrows and full black beard were white with ice.

Father staggered over to the fireplace. He plopped down into his captain's chair without even taking off his big leather boots. Slowly he began pulling off his mitts and reaching out his hands to warm them at the open hearth. Then he drew back and stared.

"The fire is almost out!" he shouted. "Kate! How many times have I told you? Never let the fire get too low."

Kate turned and gasped as she looked at the fireplace. It was true. Only a few red sparks glowed from a dull grey pile of ashes. After all the excitement with the curtains, she must have forgotten to bank the fire.

"I'm sorry!" she said as she hurried to rake the coals alive. While her father frowned at her, Kate threw on a few pieces of kindling. She picked up two larger sticks and set them aside to be ready as soon as the fire began flaming. "Sorry, Father," Kate said, turning to her father.

"Don't let it happen again," he said. He peeled off his heavy raccoon overcoat and handed it to Kate.

"Father," she said as she hung the coat on a nail by the door, "why didn't you get home last night? I was worried."

"I was tracking a deer, but when the storm came up I lost the trail and my own way, too. I decided it was best to take shelter for the night and wait for daylight. I might have just wandered farther and farther away from home."

Kate looked at her father's empty knapsack and knew he had had no luck in hunting.

"Put on some coffee and throw together a bite for me, Kate," Father said wearily as he stared into the fire. "I haven't had anything to eat since yesterday morning."

The last loaf of bread was almost gone, but Kate buttered two big slices. "There's only enough bread left for the boys to have one more piece each," she said, handing the slices to Father. "When I bake again, I'll have to crush more grain and even *it* is getting low."

"No, not our *seed*!" Father exclaimed.

Kate couldn't help feeling annoyed. What did he expect her to do? She had been very careful with the supplies. "I told you in January that I was grinding seed grain. And it takes hours to grind it in the coffee mill," she said. "It's all we have left to make flour. Our other supplies are low too."

"Well, if we must use it all, we must. So go ahead." Father ate the bread in silence. After a few minutes, he asked about the coffee.

"It'll be ready soon, Father."

"Well, could you help me with my boots in the meantime, Kate? My fingers are still numb."

Kate knelt in front of her father and unlaced the heavy boots. He pulled them off and heaved a sigh. "I had to keep moving around in my makeshift shelter all night. Otherwise I might have frozen." Father got up and moved towards his bed like a sleepwalker.

"Forget the coffee, Kate. I'm too tired now," he said. He stopped in his tracks. "What on *earth*?" he bellowed.

There on his bed sat Bobcat in a sphinx position. He opened his green eyes slowly and blinked.

"Wherever did *this* creature come from?" he exploded. Father reached out to grab him, but Bobcat sprang to the head of the bed and from there jumped easily to the rafter. His stubby tail flopped over one side of the beam as he stared down at the family from the other side.

"Alex let that poor cat in out of the storm," Kate said. "I have no idea how he got way out here."

"It looks like the wild animal Sarah Shaw was trying to pawn off on us. No ordinary cat could jump like that. And look at the size of him — and that short tail."

"I . . . I think it *is* Bobcat, but he's not really wild. He'd make a good pet for the boys."

"We have little enough food for ourselves. We'll have to get rid of him. I know your intentions were good, but really, Kate, you should never have let him in."

"But I didn't . . ."

Father sat down on his bed. "I'm going to have a few hours of shut-eye. Then I'd better see if I can pick up that deer's trail. I know it's hopeless after a storm, but . . ." He lay down. Silently, Kate picked up the boys' quilt from the captain's chair and handed it to Father. To her relief, he pulled it over himself without noticing the difference.

"Now, watch that fire!" he mumbled.

"Yes, Father," Kate sighed to herself.

A few minutes later, when Father was fast asleep, Kate crept over to the cedar chest at the foot of his bed. She reached down to the bottom and pulled out a curtain that Mother had made. Kate would make two small curtains out of it — in a hurry, before Father woke up. She was surprised he hadn't noticed the smoke in the cabin, but the fireplace always gave off a smoky smell, and Father was tired.

Kate spread out the material on the floor, took her scissors, needle, and thread from a box beside her bed, and cut the fabric in two. She laid the pieces across the table and threaded the needle. Her nimble fingers moved quickly, for her grandmother had trained her well.

Bobcat purred and swished against her leg. He'd left his perch to find out what Kate was up to.

"You must be hungry, Bobcat," Kate whispered. She tiptoed over to the cupboard, broke off a little piece of bread, and dropped it onto the floor.

The cat gobbled it down and rubbed against her again.

"Well, Bobcat, I wish you could stay. I'd love to tell Sarah about you right now."

Bobcat rubbed against her once more, then looked up at her with his head cocked to the side.

"I'm sorry, Bobcat," she said. "That's all for now."

The cat seemed to understand. He sauntered off towards the fireplace in his lopsided way and sprawled out on the bright-red hooked rug.

"Well, you do know how to make yourself at home," Kate said as she returned to her needlework. "But don't get too comfortable. As soon as Father wakes up, he'll throw you out in the snow again, and I'm afraid I won't be able to stop him."

And don't you get too used to his company, Kate warned herself sternly. She bit her lips while sewing, hurrying to finish. Once the boys woke up, it would take all her attention to keep them quiet while Father slept.

❖

"Now, boys," Father announced as he finished chewing his boiled potatoes and venison, "I'm going away again for a while." It was the middle of the afternoon. Father had slept for hours and woke up very hungry, so Kate had decided to serve supper early.

"But you just came back this morning!" Alex said.

"Yes, but I have to pick up supplies. Your sister will

take good care of you. You'll be just fine."

"Oh, yeah? She doesn't play with us," said Alex.

"And she makes us carry in wood," Ryan added.

Kate glanced over from the cupboard where she was putting away the leftovers. There were a few large chunks of venison and five potatoes. That was the last of their supplies from their cellar.

"Well, a little work won't hurt you," Father was saying. "So help your sister. Some day you'll be my big men around here."

Kate wondered what *she* would be then. Probably a broken-down old spinster.

The boys beamed back at their father and spoke at the same time.

"Can I go with you today?" Ryan shouted.

"Take me!" said Alex.

"No, not now," laughed Father. "It'll be a few years yet. But I promise you, the three of us will go hunting together when you're a little older. I can hardly wait, I tell you." Still smiling at his sons, he said, "Any dessert, Kate?"

"No, Father. I'm keeping the last bit of sugar for an emergency."

"I see. That's fine. Still it was amazing, the way your grandmother could always whip up something out of nothing. I remember her molasses pies — made out of brown sugar, molasses, and vinegar. *She* was a wonder."

Kate glared at her father, but he didn't notice.

"You should have seen the fire last night, Father. Kate and I put it out." Fiercely, Kate shook her head at Alex, but it was too late.

"What?" shouted Father. His brown eyes were alert and focused on Kate.

She tried to avoid her father's stare as she picked up the wooden bowls and stacked them on the cupboard.

"I'm waiting, Kate," he said in a solemn voice.

She turned and faced him bravely but blushed and stammered when she said, "It was an accident. The curtains caught fire from the candle."

"But how?"

"The whole cabin was rocking in the storm. It was those trees you used for cornerposts."

"The *trees* I used! That wouldn't cause a fire."

"Well, the candle slid off the table and into the curtains."

"But the table is in the middle of the room. How could it possibly . . . ?"

"I moved the table to the window. I hoped you'd see the light from the candle."

"How could I possibly see through that storm?" he said, exasperated. His brows relaxed when he saw fear in Kate's eyes. "Never mind, Kate, you meant well. Don't look so frightened. But you must learn to be more vigilant, especially when you are alone with the boys. The fire wouldn't go out so often if you spent less time dreaming."

Kate looked at the floor. Long ago, she had discovered that hard work was more bearable if she took her mind to other places — to memories of happy times with her mother, mostly — while her hands were busy. She knew it annoyed Father. Often over the years he had startled her out of a daydream with his bark. But she couldn't help it. When she was alone with the boys, she needed her dreams the most. But she could never explain this to Father.

"I realize it must be lonely for you," Father said awkwardly. Kate looked up in surprise. "And I'm afraid it may get worse. I may have to stay away a few days or even a week this time."

"A week!" Kate gulped back her fear.

"I have to be sure of getting us more food. But I've decided not to leave until tomorrow morning. We'll have time for a good talk this evening after the boys are in bed."

The rest of the day was spent in preparation. Father and Kate worked hard to stack wood indoors so it would be dry enough to use for weeks to come. Even Alex and Ryan helped by dragging one stick at a time to the house.

Finally, when the boys were asleep, Father and Kate went to the cellar and counted their supplies. When they came up, Father sat in his chair by the fireplace and Kate sat on a stool a few feet away. "I can't believe we're so low, Kate," Father said.

"I've tried to ration more, but it's hard sometimes. The boys are always hungry," Kate sighed. And so am I, she added silently.

Father looked across the room at his sleeping boys. "They do look healthy, though, so I guess they haven't suffered any . . . Well, Kate, I'm sorry to be leaving you like this. But I'll be back soon, I hope, and with food."

Kate tightened her lips and stared into the fire, frowning.

"Now cheer up, Kate. Spring is just around the corner. It's March next week. This weather can't last forever. And in the spring the men will come up from Adolphustown with food. I asked them to bring us supplies if they got any from King's Town."

Kate was trembling. "It's so hard when you're gone," she whispered. "I'm lonely and . . . afraid."

Father cleared his throat. "It's hard for all of us," he said wearily. "I'm going to bed. I'll say good-bye now because you'll be sleeping when I leave at first light tomorrow. And God willing, I'll be home before nightfall." Roughly, he patted Kate's head.

"But what if you can't get back in time, Father? What if we freeze or starve?"

"Don't talk nonsense, Kate. You'll be fine. We've managed so far, haven't we?"

Father stepped over to his sons' bed. Leaning over, he kissed each one on the forehead.

An hour later, Kate lay in her bed, still wide awake. She could hear the soft breathing of her brothers in their trundle bed beside her and the deeper breathing of her father from across the room.

A rising wind began to howl and she shivered, thinking of Bobcat. Just as she had predicted, the first thing Father had done when he woke up was throw Bobcat out into the snow. Bobcat had survived out there before, but that was no consolation. She hoped he'd found a shelter from the swirling wind and the bitter cold.

For just a moment the shrieking wind ceased and Kate heard a low, wailing meow coming from outside the door.

She held her breath and, sure enough, the sound came again.

Kate threw back her covers and tiptoed silently across the room. She hesitated at the door and stared over at Father. He had not moved, and his deep breathing continued. She lifted her hand to the door.

Kate eased back the big bolt and opened the door just a crack. A snowy nose and frosted whiskers peeped through. Kate opened the door a bit more and Bobcat squeezed through the narrow opening.

He was a quivering mass of snow and ice. His low purring seemed to catch in his throat as he stood there shaking. The poor cat took one feeble step towards Kate but moved no farther.

Kate reached down, whisked him up in her arms, and rushed over to her bed. With her bare hands, she brushed off the loose snow on his fur. She grabbed a towel from a nail at the side of her bed, wrapped him in it, and started to rub.

The poor cat seemed to be shaking even more now. Kate hopped under the covers and whisked him under the quilt next to her. He lay still for a few minutes. Then he wiggled forward until his head stuck out on the pillow next to her.

"You'd better be still," she whispered as she hung onto him. Bobcat seemed to settle down beside her. Then his eyes started to blink shut.

Kate smiled and closed her own eyes.

The wind howled wildly and the cabin swayed back and forth. But a soft purring was now added to the cabin noises as its five inhabitants slept soundly.

CHAPTER
ELEVEN

Bright light filtered through the window. It was unusually sunny today. At the table, the boys sat eating their porridge — the last of the ground oats.

"I wish we had milk for our porridge," Ryan said with his mouth full.

"Here," said Kate as she poured melted snow into the porridge. "Let's pretend this is milk."

"I like your pretend games, Kate," Alex said. "So let's pretend we're back at Albany, and you are our mother."

"We could call you Mother, couldn't we, Kate?" Ryan asked.

"No, I'd sooner not," Kate said sharply. She felt mean to answer him that way. But they hardly understood what the word "mother" meant, and she did. She would not pretend to be Mother with her brothers.

Kate got up abruptly and went over to the cupboard. It was time to start the bread, the last batch before Father came home with new supplies. Kate was counting on him coming home today or perhaps tomorrow, for he had been gone a full week.

Mornings were the hardest when, except for the hiss of the banked fire and the low breathing of her sleeping brothers, the cabin was silent. Kate longed for other sounds — the steady beat of the wooden spoon as her grandmother stirred the oatmeal cookie batter, her mother's cheerful singing as she pounded bread dough on the countertop. Now she looked forward even to Father's noisy throat-clearing, face-washing, and half-scolding encouragement to "Hurry up with that oatmeal, Kate, I'm hungry as a bear!"

Kate poured the foaming yeast from a cup and mixed in the rest of the flour and a bit of the sugar.

"Come on, Kate. Let's play pretend," Alex coaxed. "I'll pretend to be a lion and chase you all around the cabin."

"Yeah." Ryan was eager now, too. "We could both be lions. We could play Daniel in the Lion's Den — that story you tell us. You know we won't hurt you. The lions don't hurt Daniel."

"I'm busy now," Kate said as she placed the dough in an earthen bowl. She covered it with a linen towel, took it to the fireplace, and placed it on the mantel. It would begin to rise there, in the warmth of the fire.

"I want to be a *fierce* lion," Alex said. "And if we play that story, I can't be fierce." Alex started to growl loudly.

"Meow . . . meow . . ." Bobcat replied. He always did have a loud, clear meow, but this time Bobcat sounded upset. He was sitting by the door, staring back at them.

"Now look what you've done, Alex. You've scared our cat," Kate scolded.

"Hisss," shouted Alex, running towards the cat, waving his arms and wiggling his fingers. "He can be a *mean* cat. He hit me once."

"Alex!" Kate shouted.

"Meow!" Bobcat faced Alex. Then he started to pace back and forth in front of the door. His tail was twitching wildly.

"Oh, all right, Bobcat. I'll let you out if that's what you want. But Father's coming home soon, so you'd better watch out." Kate had not yet figured out an argument that might convince Father to let Bobcat stay, but she was working on it.

The cat raced outside and light streamed in through the doorway. Kate opened the door wider and breathed in the fresh air and sunshine. It was not nearly as cold as before. Kate felt her spirits lift. Today her father *would* return — she was sure of it. Why not celebrate?

"Spring is on the way," she said as she returned to the table. Her voice had a musical lilt. "After we finish our work, we can go outside to play. Now how would you like that?"

"Hooray!" both boys shouted at the same time.

"But first, you must help me with the washing," said Kate firmly. The sunshine and fresh, cold air had reminded Kate of Grandma's laundry lessons.

Grandma, and Mother, too, had insisted that clothes be dried outside, even in freezing weather. "The outside air freshens them," Grandma said. "You know, Kate, you can always tell a clean person from a dirty person by her wash on the line." Kate had complained that she didn't understand: the freshly washed clothes froze stiff and then had to be thawed out by the fire and dried inside anyway. But secretly she enjoyed the delicious outdoor smell that clung to even winter-washed bedsheets.

Kate had gathered up all the nightclothes and begun to strip her bed when she noticed the boys hadn't moved.

"Come on, then, lend a hand," she said briskly.

"We can't," whined Alex. "We're too little."

"No, you're not. I always helped Mother with the washing when I was your age. I had my own little tub and would scrub all my dolls' clothes." Kate stripped Father's bed and opened his chest to fetch out whatever needed cleaning. "Take the sheets off your bed, boys, and add them to the pile," she directed.

The twins mumbled something to each other, then Alex spoke out. "Washing is girls' work."

"That's right." Ryan was nodding his head. "And we don't want to do girls' work."

"And what makes you think it's girls' work?" Kate asked. She stared at them coldly, her hand on her hip.

"Father never does the washing," Alex explained.

"Fine," Kate snapped. "So I'll do all the work and I won't have any time left to take you outside this afternoon to play. Also, I'll be too tired to tell you stories at bedtime."

The boys looked at each other with surprise. Then Alex said slowly, "We'll help . . . I guess."

"Yeah, I guess," said Ryan.

While the boys worked, Kate rolled the two half-barrels that the boys used as stools closer to the fire. She flipped them over so they were ready to be filled and carried her largest cooking kettles over to the fire as well.

Pulling on her cape, Kate took a large bucket in each hand and opened the door. The snow shone brightly in the sunlight. She scooped her pails full, hurried inside, and emptied them into the kettles that she placed on the fire. After she had enough water warming, she'd bring in more snow for the cold rinse water. It would take a long time to prepare the water for this large washing. She almost hoped Father wouldn't arrive until late. He wouldn't be pleased to come home to a washing mess.

By noon, all the washing was done and Kate had kneaded the bread and set it back on the mantel for a second rising. Despite their complaints, the boys had enjoyed splashing about in the tubs, so much in fact that Kate had had to partially undress them to keep their clothes dry for playing outdoors later. The lines outside flapped with breeches and shirts, petticoats, and most of the family's underwear, as well as clean sheets and all their towels.

The work had made the boys and Kate hungry. They finished up the last loaf of bread, and Kate promised new bread for supper. Fortunately, the boys were too excited about going out to play to complain.

Kate was careful to dress the boys warmly, in spite of the sunshine. She didn't want them catching cold.

Clumsy with clothes, the boys waddled outside. Kate slipped quickly into her woollen cloak and thick mittens, and stepped out and around the boys.

"Look! Tracks! Maybe it's a deer," Ryan said.

Kate looked down. There was not just one set of tracks, but two. The first ones were cat tracks. The small footprints went south and around to the side of the house. The other larger footprints were apart from the others and headed towards the woods.

"Let's follow them," Ryan said, plodding along in the snow after the cat tracks.

Kate went in the opposite direction to look more closely at the larger tracks. They resembled those of a very large dog. Could they be deer tracks? She really didn't know what deer tracks looked like.

Kate looked up then and called Alex, who had moved away from them. "You'd better stay near us."

Alex turned back and tugged at the bottom of Kate's cape. "I want to make a fort. I don't want to chase any stupid cat."

"In a minute, Alex."

"Do you promise?"

"I promise."

"Oh, boy! A fort!"

Kate turned back towards the cat's trail and fell over Ryan, who had stopped directly in front of her. "Oh, Ryan, I'm sorry," she said, sitting beside him in the snowbank. Ryan rolled over and sat up laughing in the snow. His cheeks were rosy. "The cat's disappeared! Look . . . the tracks just stopped."

"The cat's a wicked witch," Alex burst out.

"What did you say, Alex?" Kate said sternly.

"That cat is really not a cat. It's a witch and it's turned itself back into a witch. That's why its tracks disappeared."

"Alex, that's a silly story," Kate said.

Ryan was staring at Kate with wide eyes. "Maybe it is a witch! Remember that story you told us about . . ."

"Meow." The unmistakable sound came from just above them. Kate looked up and laughed. There in the lower branches of one of the cabin cornerposts sat Bobcat. He was high in the tree, a long way above the cabin.

"There's your witch, boys. He looks very much like our cat to me. Come on down, Bobcat."

"Here, kitty-kitty," called Ryan. He stood up and looked high into the leafless tree.

Alex stood silently behind Kate. The three watched as the cat walked sedately along the branch and climbed down the tree to the rooftop. From there he ran across the roof and leapt with lightning speed to the snowbank, landing right next to Kate. "Let's make our fort," Alex said. "Kate, you promised." He was wading out into deeper snow not far from the forest.

Kate gave Bobcat a long stroke as he rubbed against her. Then she and Ryan followed Alex.

"This is a good spot," Alex said. "Let's make it right here." He started to roll a snowball.

They worked and played in the fresh snow, laughing as they rolled more and more snowballs and packed them together into walls for their fort. Kate's brown eyes snapped with merriment, and the sun glinted against her auburn hair. Her cheeks went rosy in the cold air and gave her a healthy glow that had not been there for weeks.

Bobcat was never far away as they worked, but he always kept his distance. After about an hour, the three sat behind their high walls of snow boulders and surveyed their work.

"Even a monster couldn't climb over that wall," Alex said with satisfaction.

"Or a witch?" Kate laughed. Just then a flying furry object came over the wall and landed in front of them.

Ryan screamed with delight and grabbed the cat. Bobcat rubbed against Ryan and purred as he was stroked.

"He's not such a bad cat," said Ryan, holding the wriggling cat tight. Alex looked at him doubtfully, then started to walk towards them. But Bobcat jumped from Ryan's arms, took a flying leap to the top of one of the fort's walls, and sat looking down at them.

Ryan laughed loudly, but Alex frowned. "I think he wants to play tag," Ryan said. He started to go after the cat, but when he came closer, Bobcat raced along the top of the wall. Then Alex started running, too.

As the boys played, Kate slipped inside to knead the bread again. This time she cut the dough into three pieces and put each piece in a pan for baking. Then she placed the pans in a row along the mantel. They would still need to rise more before she could bake them.

Stepping outside again, Kate smiled. The boys were still playing with the cat in their fort and they hadn't even missed her. She shovelled off the stoop, then sat looking at the forest. She wondered whether Father had found a deer.

The boys sank breathlessly into the deep snow. Kate felt a chill wind starting to rise. "We'd better go inside," she said. "It's starting to get cold."

"No!" said Alex. "I want to stay outside. Please. Just a little longer?"

"Please!" begged Ryan.

"Well, just a few more minutes. Then we *must*." The boys chased Bobcat along the fort wall again but they still couldn't catch him. Kate began to take down the washing.

"All right, boys, let's go in," Kate said after a few minutes. She loaded up each boy's arms with the stiffly frozen clothes and directed them indoors.

"C'mon, Bobcat," Kate said. "We're going inside now." He jumped down and picked his way through their tracks. Kate closed the door behind him.

The boys were covered with snow. Their cheeks were rosy and their damp blond bangs fell wildly over their foreheads. They looked so much happier than the timid pair who had gone outside a couple of hours before. Kate relieved them of their burdens and began to brush them off.

"I want to stay outside," Alex said. "It's no fun in here, no fun at all."

"I hate this cabin, too," said Ryan. "We never go anywhere. I want to go to town. I want to go to Albany."

"That's much too far, Ryan. Now be good boys," Kate said. "Spring will soon be here and we'll do this more often."

Kate helped them take off all their outside clothing and sent them over to the fireplace to play and warm up.

Kate looked at the bread on the mantel. The dough had risen enough to bake. She stoked the fire and placed the pans in the little oven that her father had built right into the fireplace wall. Then she spread the damp laundry all around the cabin.

The boys were stretched out on the floor in front of the fire, gazing into the flames. "I'm very hungry, Kate," Alex said.

"Me, too," said Ryan.

"The bread will be done soon," promised Kate. "And after supper Father will come home!"

The boys cheered, and Kate felt a moment's unease. What if Father didn't get back until tomorrow? Perhaps she shouldn't get the boys' hopes up.

"Let's imagine what Father will bring us," said Ryan. Kate shrugged. Oh, well, the damage was done.

"Venison!" shouted Alex. "As much as we want! And budder!"

"Candy," whispered Ryan. Kate was surprised that Ryan remembered what it was, for it had been so long since they had had any.

Apples, thought Kate. Even little, dry, withered ones would be good. Better than candy. Her stomach rumbled, and she thought she had better change the subject. She looked around and spotted Bobcat's tail, swishing back and forth from under Father's bed.

"I think Bobcat wants to play hide-and-seek," she said, and the boys ran and shouted as the cabin filled with the aroma of baking bread.

Finally the bread was ready, and as the three sat down

to eat, Kate just could not seem to stop any of them. The fresh bread tasted so good. When the meal was over she could not believe they had eaten two-thirds of the loaf. She put away the remaining bread, promising herself not to eat as much at the next meal. It was a good thing that more supplies were on the way.

Darkness gathered outside the window. Kate told the boys a story, but her own ears were alert to the sounds of Father's homecoming. Soon the boys yawned in turn, sitting on the hearth with the cat stretched out between them.

"Is Father coming soon?" asked Ryan sleepily.

"I guess not until late," said Kate. "You boys had better go to bed now."

"No! We want to stay up until Father comes!" they grumbled, but did not resist when Kate handed them their nightshirts. She made up their bed, and no sooner were their heads on the pillows than their eyes had closed.

Kate waited by the fire for another hour, then slowly banked it up with large logs for the night. It looked like Father was not coming home tonight. She made his bed anyway, then her own, her heart growing heavier with every step. She undressed and got into bed, too anxious to enjoy her clean bedding. What if Father didn't come home tomorrow, either?

The silence of the cabin was broken by a loud howling sound. Kate had heard that sound before — the first night they had come to their lot. It was certainly a wolf or wolves. Now she knew whose larger footprints had been in the snow.

Kate shivered with fear. But the single long howl did not come again. Perhaps it was only a single wolf and not a pack as before. She thought she would not be able to sleep for worrying. But the busy day had also taken its toll on her, and she finally fell into a restless sleep.

CHAPTER
TWELVE

It was not quite morning when Kate woke up to the sound of wind and snow lashing at the cabin. Hopefully, she looked over at Father's bed. It was empty. She got up stiffly in the cold and staggered over to the window in the grey darkness. Winter had returned — but Father had not.

For the next few days, Kate tried to keep herself and the boys cheerful by telling them each night, "Tomorrow, Father will be home." But she gave up when she realized it only made it harder to get up in the morning to Father's empty bed.

Kate decided to stretch out their dwindling food supplies by getting up later in the morning and going to bed earlier. That way, one tiny "meal" of bread and melted snow carried them through their short day. With the return of bad weather, there was no playing outside anyway. There was nothing for Kate to do but entertain the boys and keep the fire going.

But still, the precious bread did not last long enough. Father had been gone for two weeks when Kate shared out the last of it. She felt that something terrible must have happened to him. If not, he would have come home by now. She found it more and more difficult to calm the boys' fears, for she was not very calm herself.

With the bread gone, there was only the small amount of sugar she had kept back. She would give it to the boys a teaspoonful at a time. She would need to take one, too, sometimes, for she had to be strong to keep the fire going. The cold seemed to be coming through new cracks. Perhaps the shaking cornerposts had loosened some mud chunks between the logs.

On the morning of the second day without food, Kate lay in bed and despaired. Outside, the trees creaked and the wind moaned. For a fleeting moment, Kate imagined making snowshoes and heading straight to the Shaws'. But Father might be too weak when he returned to travel farther. She and the boys would have to stay put.

Kate stared up to the rafters. The frost-coated nails of the roof stared stonily down at her. After a while, she drifted back into a light sleep and an hour later woke to the sound of Bobcat meowing noisily beside her bed.

"What's wrong with you, Bobcat? You know you can go and use the sandbox now." Bobcat kept meowing.

"All right, Bobcat, all right," she said as she got out of bed, flung on her cloak, and opened the door. The snow had stopped, and the sky was beginning to clear. But the snowbank outside the cabin was now almost six feet high. The cat hesitated, then stared at Kate. "Oh, all right," said Kate. She put on her boots, got the shovel from beside the door, and scooped out a path. Bobcat followed her for a while, then hopped up onto the packed snow and darted off towards the forest. He did not fall through the surface of the snow because he was so light.

"Be careful, Bobcat," Kate called gently after him. She knew he might not always be able to walk on top of the snow. She could just picture him falling into a hole so deep that even *he* could not jump or claw his way out. Would she and her brothers find his stiff body in the spring, just yards from the front door? No. He was more apt to be eaten by a hungry, howling wolf. But it was probably better for him to leave. She could not feed him, and out there he would have a chance.

Shivering, Kate went over to the fireplace, sank into her father's chair, and pushed off her boots. She reached over, put a stick of light cedar on the coals, and watched it quickly blaze up. At least it had stopped snowing. She could bring in wood all day — or at least until she had every corner of the house filled. Another storm could easily come and before long she would be too weak to carry wood.

"Kate," Alex called. She turned suddenly, for she had thought both boys were sleeping. He was sitting up in bed, staring over at her.

"Yes, Alex," she said.

"I'm hungry, Kate." He looked up at her pitifully with his big blue eyes.

Kate swallowed. "I'll bring you a sugar drink," she promised. "And how would you like me to tell you a story? Come on over to the fire where it's warm." She patted her lap. She didn't want to wake Ryan.

Alex slid off his bed, but when his feet hit the planks, he seemed to buckle and he nearly fell to the floor. "Carry me, Kate," he said. His blue eyes seemed clouded. Kate walked over and pulled him up in her arms. He feels hot, she thought as she carried him over to the chair and plopped him down.

"You sit here, Alex," she said, "while I get you that sugar drink I promised. It'll help you feel better."

Kate mixed water with sugar and a pinch of mustard. The mustard would warm him and help him fight a chill.

"Here, Alex," Kate said. "Drink this. There's a whole spoonful of sugar in it."

"I don't want to drink anything. I just want to have some porridge." Kate felt sudden tears rise in her eyes, and blinked them back. The boys had never liked their porridge, but Father had made them eat it. Now Alex was crying for it.

"Drink the water and I'll tell you a story." Kate tipped the cup of water to her brother's lips. He put both hands around the cup and sipped slowly at first. Then he started to gulp the drink down.

"That's good, Kate. I'll take another cup."

"In a while," she said, trying to put him off. She set the empty cup beside the chair and picked Alex up and wrapped him in a warm quilt from her own bed.

Sitting in the captain's chair with her arms wrapped around her brother, she began, "Once upon a time, there was a little boy called David. He lived with . . ."

"I like this story," said Alex, turning his head and looking up at Kate. "The best part is where David uses his slingshot to kill the horrible giant."

"So David lived with his parents and brothers," Kate continued, "but he was very lonely, for he had to go out to the fields to . . ."

"David was a shepherd," interrupted Ryan from across the room. He was sitting up in bed now, listening to the story. "He used to watch the sheep all by himself out in the fields."

"That's right, Ryan, and sometimes he had real problems."

"Yes, one day a lion came by and . . ." Alex started.

"And grabbed a lamb," said Ryan. "But David chased the lion and pulled its mane so it dropped the little lamb. Another time a big bear got one of the lambs. But David got it back."

"And how was David able to do all that?" Kate asked.

Alex roused and stared over at Ryan, who said, "David prayed for God to help him. Then he took a huge club and beat back the bear and the lion. He beat both of them."

"Yes, David said that God delivered him out of the paw of the lion and out of the . . ."

"Paw of the bear," yawned Ryan.

"Be quiet," said Alex. "Kate's telling the story."

"But I can . . ."

"Come on over here, Ryan," Kate said. Ryan walked over, dragging his quilt behind him, and sat down in front of the fireplace with his hands and feet open to the warmth.

"Oh, boy," said Alex when Kate finished the story, "some day, I'd like to fight a giant."

We don't have to fight giants to know that God can take care of us — like right now, Kate thought, but she said nothing to the boys. She didn't want them to think about their own troubles. It would be better to let them keep thinking about David. Kate carried Alex over to his bed, then turned to Ryan. "Now, Ryan, you stay right there where it's warm, and I'll fix you a cup of sugar water."

Ryan smiled and wiggled his bare toes to the fire. "Isn't it funny, Kate," he said. "My bare toes are warm but my back is cold."

Kate was glad that Ryan didn't seem as weak as his brother. But then Ryan always slept more, so she supposed he was more rested. Alex had tossed and turned all night. She looked over, and sure enough, Alex had slipped off to sleep again.

Kate handed her brother the cup and pulled the quilt more tightly around his shoulders. Ryan looked up wistfully. His big blue eyes looked even larger in his thin face.

"You'd better drink your sugar water," Kate said.

"Aren't we going to give thanks this morning?" he said. "We always give thanks, Kate."

"Of course," Kate swallowed. "I forgot. You go ahead, Ryan."

Ryan leaned his head down and began. "Thank you for the sugar water. Please bring Father home soon with lots of stuff. Amen."

Kate's eyes filled. She turned towards the window so that Ryan could not see her tears. She wondered how much longer she could stand this waiting and for what . . . to die? Were she and her brothers really and truly going to starve to death?

Still there was something she could do. She would take the small hatchet and tear bark off a nearby tree. They could suck the bark. Kate stared at the forest. Even in the daylight, it looked dark and cold. But it was going to be a bright day, and she would not have to go far. Would a wolf come prowling out of the shadows?

"Ryan," she said. "Could you take care of Alex while I go into the woods and cut a little bark from the trees?" She knew that people back in Albany used to make beer from the bark of spruce trees. Her father claimed it kept them from getting scurvy. "If we could boil a little bark in water, it might taste nice."

Ryan made a face. "I don't think I'd like it, Kate. I'd rather keep drinking the sugar water."

Kate did not have the heart to tell him that the sugar would soon be gone. She put a log on the fire and dressed in her warmest clothes. "Now you must not come outside. And don't let Alex come out if he wakes up. You watch from the window. I'll keep right in sight — most of the time, anyway."

Ryan stood by the door, watching her closely. "I don't think this is a good idea, Kate," he said. His bottom lip quivered.

Kate squatted down and wrapped both arms around him. "I'll not go far. You can watch me from the window."

"But what if a bear or a wolf comes out of the forest? What will you do then, Kate?"

"I'll pray — just like David did."

"Could we pray *before* you go?" he asked.

"Yes," she said in a quiet voice with her arms still around her brother. "Please, God," she began with a lump in her throat. She could not continue. She buried her face against him.

"Take care of Kate," said Ryan all in one breath. He opened his eyes and looked up at Kate. "You'll be fine now." *He* seemed to feel better anyway, Kate thought.

She wished she could be so certain. She picked up a bucket from beside the door and tied it around her waist with some twine. Then she walked out into the fresh air. She stepped cautiously towards the forest, testing each foothold. The sun was shining brightly and the snow was becoming much softer. Even the wind had died down. A couple more weeks like this, she thought, and spring would be just around the corner.

At the edge of the forest, Kate turned and looked back. She waved at the small face pressed to the window.

Passing out of the sunshine into the shadows of the thick evergreen trees, fear gripped her. She could hear the snapping of twigs from farther on in the woods. She wondered if wolves would be out this early in the morning. And what about bears? Was it soon enough for them to be coming out of hibernation?

Kate cut a sharp notch into each tree as she walked into the thicker growth. That way she'd be able to find her way home.

When she came upon a spruce tree, she slashed the bark, chipping pieces loose and dumping them into the bucket. She couldn't help wondering again about Bobcat.

Maybe he was watching her from a nearby tree.

When the bucket was almost full, she turned and looked for the small hatchet nicks on the bark of the trees. For a minute, she froze. She couldn't see one mark. In the frightening whiteness, all directions looked the same. Kate reached out and touched the rough bark of a maple tree to her left. There was no notch on that one. Nor was there any mark on the tree ahead of her. So she turned around. Still no marks.

Her heart was thumping so loudly she was sure any animal in the forest would be able to hear it. Then she thought of little Ryan's voice saying, "Please, God, take care of Kate," and she remembered how God had kept back the paw of the lion and the paw of the bear from David and his sheep. She added her own prayer and went ahead with more confidence, looking for the trail.

A blue jay screamed above Kate's head. As she looked up, she saw the sun out of the corner of her eye. Thank you, blue jay, she said to herself, though the bird was unaware of her plight. If not for that scream, she would never have looked up and seen the sun in the southeast. Now that she knew where southeast was, Kate turned north and soon found a nick in a willow not far from where she was standing. She flew back along the trail, swinging her bucketful of bark, thinking about how she would tell Sarah about her adventure. Lost in the woods and rescued again — not far from where they had met up with a bear.

Kate came to the edge of the forest, sighing with relief. But as she went to step into the clearing, she froze.

There before her eyes in the snow, the bare bones of an animal were sticking out. Were they the bones of a deer killed by a wolf? Or had a wolf been killed by a bear? Surely it was a deer, for a patch of brown skin matched that of a deer. Then she saw the same dog-like footprints that she had seen weeks ago near their cabin. It must be a wolf's prints — certainly not a bear. Was that wolf lurking nearby?

When she broke through the edge of the woods, the sun was shining brightly. It must be mid-morning now. She'd taken longer than she'd thought. In the clear light, she could see two frightened faces in the window of the cabin.

She started to run, but just as she reached the stoop, she turned and looked back to the woods. In the very spot where she had stood a few seconds before, there was a wolf. He was a full three feet high and his tail stretched straight behind him. He boldly began pacing towards the cabin; his grey-white hair seemed to cling to the sides of his gaunt body. He's starving, too, Kate thought as she stared back at the animal. Then his black, rubbery nose twitched, and his lips curled back, exposing his long front fangs.

Kate saw his green eyes roll up to her in a wild, weird stare. For a few seconds, the wolf and the girl held each other in a fixed gaze. Then the wolf started to streak towards Kate. She turned and jumped up onto the stoop.

Pounding on the door, she screamed, "Let me in!"

The door opened almost instantly. Alex burst out to grab her, "The door wasn't locked."

Pushing Alex ahead of her, Kate almost fell inside. She slammed the door shut and pulled the bolt across to make it more secure. She leaned against it gasping.

"I saw that wolf!" shouted Alex. "I was scared!"

Ryan clung to his sister. "Oh, Kate, will he come through the window?"

"Oh, no!" said Kate. "He'll go away." She took off her cloak, walked over to the window, and gave a deep sigh of relief. "Look, he's gone already."

The boys rushed to the window.

"But he looked so awful," said Alex.

"Did you get anything, Kate?" asked Ryan.

"Yes, I've got a lot of nice bark! I'm going to boil it in water to make us a sweet drink."

"Bark!" Alex pouted. "Yuck. I thought you were going to catch a rabbit or a wild hen or something."

"I was praying you'd catch a wild turkey," Ryan said wistfully. "I'd like roast turkey for supper."

Alex stared at the bark in the bucket. "Looks like *wood*," he said. "I don't want to eat wood. Wood's for burning."

"You'll see how good this new drink will be," Kate said, also trying to convince herself.

"How long will it take you to make it?" Alex asked.

"I don't really . . ." Kate did not finish the sentence, for she did not know a thing about making beer, the kind that kept away scurvy. She supposed she'd just boil it in water. At least it couldn't hurt them. Or could it? She sank weakly into the captain's chair.

The trip into the woods had tired her out. She tried

not to think of the wolf nearby and all the wood she must bring in before nightfall.

Ryan and Alex came over and sat at Kate's feet. "When's Father coming home?" Ryan asked. His eyes were sad and listless.

"I miss him, Kate," said Alex.

"Oh, he'll be home any day now. He's probably caught a big buck and it's taking him all this time to cut and pack it to haul home." Kate looked into the flames to avoid the boys' eyes.

"And now Bobcat has gone, too," Ryan said. "I hunted everywhere in here for him while you were gone and I couldn't find him."

Kate gulped. "Yes, he's gone," she said. "He left early this morning. I had to let him go because we didn't have any food for him, and he wanted to go." She could not stand to think of Bobcat out there with that wolf.

"I miss him," Ryan sighed. Alex said nothing, but Kate saw a tear in one of his eyes.

After a silence, Kate said, "Now, boys, you have a rest while I bring in the wood. Then I'll tell you another story."

They did not object. They sat in Father's chair and waited quietly — too quietly — while she got ready to go out again.

Kate staggered over to the door and listened carefully. Very slowly she drew it open a few inches and peeked outside.

Then she pulled it wide open.

There was no sign of the wolf. But in her mind's eye, those green eyes were still burning into hers.

CHAPTER
THIRTEEN

It took Kate all afternoon to fill every corner of the cabin with wood. She was so weak from lack of food that she could only manage small loads. She walked slowly and as she rested often, she looked about her for signs of the wolf. She did not know if she would be able to run to the cabin fast enough. But she did know that they must have the much-needed fuel. Still, waves of dizziness made her stumble and drop pieces of wood. The boys were not in her way. They were too weak to come outside.

When she was done, she hardly had the strength to deal with the bark she had gathered earlier. With a sharp knife, she stripped the cream-coloured, clean inner bark from the woody outer bark. She cut it into small pieces and dropped them into a pot of water. When it had simmered for a while, she filled two mugs and added a small spoon of sugar to each.

"Here you go, boys — spruce tea!" announced Kate. The boys peered into their mugs doubtfully.

"Where's yours, Kate?" Ryan asked.

"Oh, I don't want any just now. I'll have mine later,"

she said. She planned to have hers in the morning so she'd have the strength to begin the day's tasks.

After they'd finished, Kate led them over to Father's captain's chair. "Now what story would you like tonight?" Kate asked as they huddled together.

Thump! Something was on the front stoop.

"It's Father!" shouted Alex, sliding off the chair.

"Meow!"

"It's Bobcat!" yelled Ryan.

"It's Father *and* Bobcat!" said Alex.

Both boys rushed over to the door, but Ryan got there first. He flung back the bolt and Alex opened the door.

It was not Father . . . but Bobcat was there. Though he was shivering and covered with snow, he was making a happy purring sound. On the stoop in front of him was a rabbit — a thin one, but full grown and much bigger than Bobcat himself.

"Bobcat! You caught us some supper!" Kate scooped up the rabbit and the cat staggered inside.

"Bobcat! Our hero!" Ryan reached for the cat.

"Leave him alone, Ryan," Kate said quickly. "He's tired. Here, you make him a bed by the fire with these rags and I'll fix us a rabbit dinner!"

While Ryan made a nest on the mat in front of the fireplace, Kate carried the rabbit over to the cupboard.

"Can I . . . can I take care of Bobcat, too?" Alex asked.

"Of course you can, Alex. He'd love it," Kate said, taking a knife off the rack above the cupboard.

Kate quickly skinned the rabbit, keeping her knife on the sinews between the fur and the meat, the way she'd

seen Father do it. She threw Bobcat some of the insides
and he gobbled them up greedily. She cut the meat into
strips and pushed three pieces onto a long fork and held
them over the fire. The meat smelled delicious as it
sizzled over the flames.

The boys sat cross-legged before the fireplace, watching anxiously. Their eyes were sparkling for the first time
in days.

In minutes, the three of them were chewing the
savoury meat. "Mmm," said Alex.

"It's better than roast turkey," said Ryan. "Here,
Bobcat, you have some, too!"

"I wouldn't give him any more, Ryan," Kate said as
she took tiny bites of her piece in an effort to make it last
longer. "Bobcat is pretty full, I think. He's eaten a lot of
the insides and he likes raw meat best anyway."

"More!" cried Alex, his mouth full.

"Yeah, let's have more," Ryan smiled.

Kate knew she should boil the rest and store it in the
cellar, but she was so ravenous herself, she couldn't say
no. Maybe Bobcat would catch another rabbit tomorrow.
She quickly grabbed some more strips and roasted them.

An hour later she regretted her generosity. Both Ryan
and Alex threw up everything they had eaten, and Kate
herself felt queasy. It had been so long since they had had
fresh meat, their stomachs weren't used to it. She wiped
the boys' faces, gave them some more spruce tea, and
settled them in bed.

Before she went to sleep, Kate cut the rest of the
rabbit in chunks and put it into the pot, bones and all.

Cooked slowly all night, it would make a rich stew that would last them a few days.

For the first time in over a week, Kate was hopeful.

◇

Every day for the next two weeks, Bobcat went hunting. Once he brought only a skinny mouse, which Kate made him keep. But on all the other days, he caught a rabbit and laid it on the cabin floor. Most times they were thin, but the meat was good. Kate thought Bobcat must be enjoying some good meals, too, because he was filling out a little. He was probably eating mice or birds in the woods.

Life was almost cheery in the cabin during those weeks. The boys shouted and wrestled, and when they got too noisy, Kate sent them out to play in the snow close to the cabin. She was too happy to scold them, for she saw them feeling like their old selves.

Kate was building up a reserve of smoke-dried rabbit meat. And she was planning what the family would eat after the snow melted. In the early spring, there would be sap from the maple trees and later there would be fiddleheads. Mother used to pick them back in Albany before they turned into ferns. Then she would fry them in the iron spider frying pan over the fire.

Now that she was eating better, Kate's spirits began to rise. She imagined picking wild berries in the woods with Sarah and laughing about the winter's adventures. They would even let Betsy and Alex and Ryan come into the fern glade to play while they picked strawberries to make pies.

In the middle of the last week of March, Kate woke up from a sound sleep to feel the wind rocking the cabin again. She got out of bed and shivered over to the window. It was snowing — and not gently. It was a blizzard. The white snow was beating against the window and the wind was screaming through the trees. Kate turned away, went back to bed, and cried softly into her pillow.

Stop sniffling, Kate, she said to herself at last. The winter is almost over. This will be the last big snowstorm. Before he had left, Father had hired someone in Adolphustown to come out to the cabin in the spring with supplies. That would be a relief.

The next morning, even Bobcat knew they were snowbound. He stared up at the snowdrift rising against the window, turned around, and flopped down on the mat in front of the fireplace.

On the third morning of the storm, the wind stopped. A bank of snow had risen nearly to the top of the window. Kate carefully raised the sash and reached out one hand to brush the snow off the sill. An avalanche of fresh snow fell from the window and let in a little light, but a whole pile fell right into the cabin.

"Oh, good, lots of snow — and it's inside!" Alex shouted, leaping from his bed. "C'mon, Ryan, let's make a fort!"

"No, Alex!" Kate shouted, but it was too late. Alex and Ryan were shuffling around in the snow, scooping up bits and making a wall. A large puddle formed near the door.

Sighing, she collected some rags to clean it up.

Bobcat joined her at the door, twitching his tail and meowing loudly. Kate ignored him at first. She was afraid to open the door for fear of starting an avalanche. But Bobcat persisted and his meowing got louder.

"Oh, all right," Kate said. "But you'll have to go out the window." She lifted the sash as high as it would go.

She gasped at the drifts. Between the cabin and the trees, some of the snowbanks were eight feet high.

"No, Bobcat," she said as the cat hopped up onto the windowsill. "It's too deep." But even as she spoke, Bobcat took a mighty leap outside and landed far beyond her reach. Then he disappeared around the side of the cabin. "Be careful, Bobcat!" she called out.

Kate wished Bobcat had not gone out when the snow was so deep. He might hunt all day and find nothing. Or worse, he might fall into a gap between snowbanks and not be able to get out. She hoped the wolf was buried in the snow.

She felt two small bodies next to her as she reached up to pull down the sash. "We'd better pray for Bobcat," said Ryan. "Remember David's little lambs."

It was as if Ryan had read her thoughts.

CHAPTER FOURTEEN

The following morning, Bobcat had not returned. The sky was beginning to cloud over again, and the wind was picking up. Ryan was very worried. He stood crying at the window.

Kate felt like crying herself, but she knew it would not help any of them. Maybe a new game would cheer them up, she thought.

"Ryan! Alex! Both of you! I have an important job for you!" She fetched two spoons from the cupboard and handed them to the boys. "I want you to dig through the dirt on the cellar floor and look for some buried treasure."

The boys looked at each other with excitement.

"What kind of treasure, Kate?" asked Ryan.

"Gold," said Kate. "I'm wondering if maybe we missed a carrot or two."

"That's not treasure," said Alex scornfully.

"I bet I find one first!" said Ryan. Alex couldn't resist the challenge and rushed to the ladder. All three went down together, and while the two boys were digging furiously, Kate collected the rest of the roasted rabbit. After that was gone, only a little dried meat remained.

Kate left the boys to their game, put on her cloak, and went outside with the shovel. Yesterday she had begun to shovel a path, but had only managed to get a foot from the door. She had only been working ten minutes when she heard shouts. She dropped her shovel and ran inside.

"We found some, Kate!" shouted Ryan.

"I found mine first!" shouted Alex.

"You did not," argued Ryan.

"Well done, both of you," interrupted Kate before the argument turned into another fight. She was surprised and pleased. She hadn't really thought there was anything more to be found. "Now get on your cloaks and help me dig out a path."

The boys put their spoons and the two small, dried-out carrots on the table and hurried into their cloaks.

"I want to use the shovel, Kate," said Alex, as she fastened his cloak tightly at his neck with a hawthorn needle.

Kate answered quickly. "You may each have a turn, and since you asked first, you may have the first turn."

With a whoop, Alex ran outside. Kate wondered where he got his energy. The little bit of shovelling she had done had exhausted her. Even Ryan wriggled impatiently while she fastened his cloak. Wearily, she let him pull her along to the door as fast as he could go in his heavy boots.

A gust of wind came over the top of the wall of snow and a pile of it fell on Kate and Ryan as they came through the doorway. Kate brushed the snow from Ryan's hat and looked ahead for Alex. In that second, a whole chunk of the snow wall he was digging at caved in — right on top of him. He disappeared before her unbelieving eyes. Only one blue mitt stuck out above the heavy pile of snow that filled the path.

Kate ran towards the mitt and yanked at it, but Alex's hand had disappeared. The shovel was buried with him, so she clawed frantically at the snow with her mitten-covered hands. Then she threw off her mittens and clawed with her bare hands and arms.

Ryan pulled and punched the snow beside her. In a few minutes, they had uncovered Alex's hand and arm. When they reached his face, he was crying and panting in fear. The snow had not filled in tightly around him, so he had been able to get some air.

"You're fine, Alex. We'll have you out soon," Kate said.

In a few more minutes, they had him free of the snow.

"Now follow me carefully," said Kate, taking Alex by the hand. She eyed the walls of snow on either side nervously.

"No, I'm scared. It's too far!"

"Don't be scared, Alex, I'll protect you."

"I can't," Alex whimpered. "Carry me, Kate." Kate scooped him up in her arms and was surprised at how heavy he felt. I must be weaker than I thought, she said to herself as she staggered along. Ryan clung to her coat, dragging the shovel behind him.

As they entered the cabin, the sky began to darken.

Was it late in the day, or was another storm coming? Kate wondered. She plopped Alex down in front of the fireplace and Ryan knelt beside him. Together, they pulled off his clothes. He had no energy to do it himself.

Finally, the twins were each in their warm night-clothes and they had all had something to eat. Kate filled a pot with water to brew some bark tea. Then she swept the floor.

When she had finished, Kate sat for a while in Father's chair. The boys had fallen asleep together on the mat. Their blond hair had grown long, and now it flopped over their eyes and around their shoulders. Kate was so tired she longed to lie down there and fall asleep beside them. But she had one task left to do before bedtime. She *had* to go outside and clear the snowslide out of the path so Bobcat could reach the cabin. Surely he would come tonight. If only he would bring them a rabbit — no matter how thin it was.

Kate threw the snow cautiously from the path so she would not start another avalanche. Dusk was starting to close in around her. In a while, she began to think she was being silly to keep on. Bobcat would surely jump over the pile. She mustn't be thinking clearly to be out here shovelling for a cat who could jump to the roof.

Kate gave a low, tired laugh and leaned on her shovel, looking straight along the path. The snow glistened in the dusk — except for one dark spot on the ground near the forest.

Bobcat? Kate stared again.

She stuck the shovel in the snowbank and, testing each

foothold, climbed over the snowslide. She plodded through the drifts towards the spot.

A few feet away, she recognized Bobcat. One leg lay sprawled to the side as though it was broken, and a little trail of blood showed along the snow behind him. Kate stared in horror for a minute before falling to her knees. Bobcat opened an eye partway and gave a faint squeak that was not quite a meow.

"You're alive," she mumbled softly. "Oh, Bobcat." He did not move at all. She reached out her hand to pet his head but drew it back, afraid that she might hurt him.

She whipped off her cloak and laid it flat on the snow beside him. She slowly raised the less-bloody side of his body a little and pulled the cloak under it. With her hand under the shoulder on that side, she pulled him fully onto the woollen cloak.

Holding the outer corners of her cloak, she lifted him and carried him down the pathway.

She tapped the toe of her boot against the door. She had left the boys sleeping by the fireplace and really didn't think they would wake up and hear. But she waited anyway, then tried again.

Just as she was deciding to put Bobcat down and open the door, it swung wide and there stood Ryan. His little face went ashen as he looked at Kate and the cat. Behind him, Kate could see Alex in bed. He must have moved while I was out shovelling, she thought.

"Is Bobcat dead . . . ?" he asked.

"Bobcat's been hurt, but he's not dead . . . Now close the door. It's getting colder."

Kate laid Bobcat down in front of the fireplace. Ryan knelt beside her, and tears began streaming down his face. "Oh, Bobcat, Bobcat, I love you, I love you," he kept repeating in a choked voice.

Kate's throat tightened, but she knew she could not cry — not in front of Ryan. "I think he's going to be all right," she said. "Now let me look at him. You get into bed with Alex now." She tried to push Ryan back a little. He squeezed over to make room for her next to the cat, but he would not leave.

She took a closer look at Bobcat's leg. The bleeding had stopped, and the bones did not look displaced. Heavy claw marks stood out on his back, but the bleeding had stopped there, too.

"He looks awful, Kate," Ryan groaned. "Just awful."

"But he isn't meowing or crying or anything," Kate said. "Maybe it looks worse than it is."

"Maybe," he said. "But can't we do something, Kate?" He looked up tearfully at his sister.

"It'll be best to let him alone for tonight. Maybe in the morning we can wash his wounds." Kate thought she might start more bleeding if she tried to clean him now. And with no flour to put on the open veins, she would be unable to stop the bleeding if it started.

"He's chilled to the bone and needs lots of heat," Kate said. "I think I'll sleep over here by the fireplace where I'll be handy to keep the fire going."

"I'll stay, too," said Ryan. He lay down beside Bobcat with his head on the edge of Kate's bloody cape.

Bobcat meowed quietly.

"Did you hear that, Kate?" Ryan burst out. "He spoke to me!"

"Yes, he did. And that's because he's getting better. So now you can get into bed with your brother." Ryan shook his head.

"Well, all right. You rest beside him while I get ready for bed."

She built up the fire, then changed into her night-clothes. She grabbed her pillow and quilts and curled up on the mat next to Ryan and the cat. In a few minutes, she sank into a light sleep.

A few hours later when Kate woke, she lifted the sleeping Ryan, laid him softly into his bed beside Alex, and drew up the quilts tightly around both of them. Then she put two sticks on the fire and dropped into her own bed.

Out of habit, she kept waking to feed the fire. Each time she added a stick, she expected to find that Bobcat had stopped breathing. But he fought on. He was a plucky cat, she thought. If anyone could make it, he could.

In the morning, Ryan woke first and came over to check on Bobcat. "He's alive," he choked out, "but . . ."

Kate heated some water, added a little salt, and, slowly and carefully, washed each of Bobcat's wounds. His leg wound opened and bled, but Kate dabbed at it gently and it stopped. She expected he would struggle, but he lay still. With broadcloth, she tightly bound the leg that hung down so strangely. When Kate was done, the boys offered Bobcat a little of the bark water and tiny pieces of rabbit meat. But he didn't touch them. Kate hoped there was nothing wrong with his insides, for then there was nothing she could do to help him.

At noon, Kate gave Alex and Ryan some bits of dried meat while she drank bark water. After eating, the boys went back to Bobcat. In a low voice, Ryan said, "Bobcat, we love you." Silently, Alex put his thin arm around Ryan's shaking shoulders.

Later that day, Kate staggered outside to bring in more wood. She knew she must, for the inside supply was running low. The cold outside air seemed to pierce right through her cloak even though the sun was shining and the wind had gone down. But she was thankful that the outside woodpile was lower now, and it was not as hard to reach the sticks.

She plodded back and forth carrying only a few sticks. Inside, she dropped them into a heap in the middle of the floor. When she finally looked up to rest, she saw that her brothers had fallen fast asleep. Even the sound of the wood crashing onto the floor did not wake them.

Kate kept going for wood until the light started to fade away and she was too weak to go out one more time. She must not fall in the snow because she might not be able to get up. And she had to feed the fire.

Finally she pushed the big door closed and, struggling, pulled the bolt across. With her coat still on, she stumbled over to Father's chair and sank into it.

Kate looked down and saw that Bobcat had roused. He was gingerly licking his wounded leg, and the bark water was lower in the dish. Kate bent over and stroked him lightly behind his ear.

"You poor, poor cat," she said.

She concentrated on how sore Bobcat must be feeling. That way, she did not have to think about what they were going to do for food now that their trusty hunter could no longer hunt.

CHAPTER
FIFTEEN

Three days passed. Bobcat recovered bit by bit. On the fourth day, he seemed ready to eat. But by then, all the meat was gone.

Once again, Kate had to feed the boys sugar water. There was so little sugar left, Kate drank only bark tea. It was bitter, but at least the warmth was comforting.

On the fifth day after Bobcat's return, Alex woke and stared at Kate with clouded eyes. "Water. I want a drink of water."

Kate went to the cupboard and brought over a cup of cold spruce tea. Ryan woke up, too, and stared up at Kate. To each boy in turn she offered the bitter liquid, and they drank without complaining.

"Look," Kate said, trying to rouse them. "Bobcat woke up for a few minutes and walked around."

"I'm glad," Ryan said, but his voice was dull. "I don't want to get out of bed, Kate. I'm so tired."

She didn't argue. She didn't feel like leaving her bed, either, but she had to keep feeding the fire. What if she became too weak to keep it burning? She looked at the boys, huddled close together under their covers. The cabin seemed colder these days, even with a blazing hearth. What would it be like *without* a fire?

Thinking about it, a chilling horror filled her. Please, God, what do I do? she asked silently.

A thought came to her.

"Boys. Ryan, Alex," she said gently. They opened their eyes. "Sit up, please." They watched as she gathered up all their spare clothing. Their bodies were limp as she dressed them in as much of it as possible: two knitted coats, two pairs of breeches, three pairs of heavy socks, and a knitted toque on each of their heads. If it got colder, she would add their boots, outdoor capes, and mitts.

When she was done, Kate went over to the two buckets of bark water and dipped out another bowlful for Bobcat. He was up now and lapping a little from the dish beside him. Then she got an even bigger bowl and set it out in case he needed more.

She drank a big cupful herself. Maybe it would give her strength. Then she set both buckets near the boys' bed and left a tin dipper floating on top.

After that, she was exhausted. Like a sleepwalker, she stumbled over to Father's chair and fell into it.

❖

Kate woke with a start. The fire was very low. She tried to rise but couldn't. Maybe she was still asleep and dreaming that she couldn't move. She looked over to the window. Was that a huge bear covering the window with his big, black body? Kate screamed — a dry croak that woke her fully. She pushed herself slowly up out of the chair.

The wind and the cold and the nighttime darkness pressed against the cabin window, trying to get in. The glow and warmth from the fire had faded, and Kate had to feel her way across the floor to the wood sticks. She came back with a stick, pushed it into the centre of blackened coals with a fire iron, and watched and waited for it to ignite. The fire was so weak, she did not dare add another stick until she saw the first burning brightly. Her eyes closed, but she forced them open. She must keep awake. She must feed the fire. She went to the woodpile and slowly dragged over three more sticks to have them ready.

When the fire was going well, Kate threw in several sticks and the biggest log she could carry. She stayed there until it was blazing, then went over to her own bed, crawled in, and pulled all her quilts up and over her head. Dark shadows seemed to close in around her. She would have liked to light a candle, but she was too tired. She soon fell into a deep sleep.

"Kate! Kate!" Alex peered anxiously into her face. "You were making scary sounds, Kate. I brought you some bark water."

A thin ray of sunlight glinted through a hole in the windowpane that Alex had scratched free of frost. He offered her the dipper. She struggled up onto one elbow and reached for it. Then she noticed that Alex had on all his outdoor clothes except for his mitts. She looked over at the fireplace. It was completely black.

She fell out of bed and crawled to the hearth as fast as she could. She reached for a fire iron and raked the coals desperately. Thanks be to God! A few coals still glowed underneath like red jewels. She dragged them to the top and threw in some birchbark and kindling she had set aside for an emergency. She sat in Father's chair to wait for it to ignite.

"You didn't drink your bark water," said Alex. His hand trembled as he offered her the dipper again.

She took a few sips and handed it back. "Thank you," she said softly. Together they watched as the fire caught and began to blaze. Kate added a big chunk of wood.

"Kate, I'm scared. Can I come into bed with you?" Alex stared at her, his eyes enormous in his thin white face, and Kate had a peculiar feeling. Sometime long ago, when they were well-fed and happy and Father was only a wagon-length away, Alex had asked this same question. She felt tears come, but swallowed them down.

"Of course," she answered. "Let's get Ryan, too. It will be warmer that way." She put her arm around his thin shoulders and they leaned on each other as they walked back to her bed.

◇

Again Kate woke from a troubled sleep to a freezing cold cabin. She wanted to get up to tend the fire but couldn't move. She stared straight up to the rafters. The frosted nails of the roof turned into a multitude of glistening eyes staring fiercely down upon her. She could hear the wind roaring in the darkness and the heavy ice-laden branches slashing against the cabin, now in motion again.

A thunderous crash of something hitting the roof jolted her back to reality. The impact came crunching down almost upon them, and she felt a blast of cold snow all around her and her brothers. The loud banging continued and came into the cabin. She threw herself over the boys to protect them. Was the whole cabin caving in? Were they being buried alive in snow and splintered logs?

They had been cold before, but now with the snow and wind blowing right over and around them, she knew they would freeze. She reached out her hand from under the quilts and touched her brothers' chilly faces. Even the three of them together couldn't keep the bed warm.

She lay still and prayed silently while the storm continued to crash around them. The snow fell steadily over them as the wind grew calmer. The bed even started to feel a little warm. Kate slipped back into a deadly sleep full of nightmares about bears and wolves.

Kate woke when she heard knocking. She shook off a load of snow as she flung back the blanket and opened her eyes. She saw light, a lot of light, coming in from above. She looked straight ahead to where the door had been. It was gone. Instead there was a huge pile of snow all the way to the open roof. It had sharp pieces of wood sticking out of it. She would never be able to get around to the door to open it. Was she awake or still dreaming?

She heard the sounds again.

"Father!" she called out. There was no answer, but the banging came again. She was not dreaming. But where was the door?

Then something or someone jumped down from above and onto the top of the pile of wood and snow in front of the door. Kate shrank in fear as she looked at the dark, fur-covered figures crouched there staring down at her and Alex and Ryan! To her fevered eyes, they looked like the bear and the wolf of her dreams. The bear's eyes moved from Kate to the faces of her brothers.

"Aaah!!!" Kate screamed. Darkness closed in around her as she passed out.

PART THREE

❖

Out of the Storm

CHAPTER
SIXTEEN

Kate woke up to the sound of someone singing.

"*Ah ho weya weya howeya he.*
Ah ho weya weya howeya he."

She did not understand the words but they were gentle and soothing. She had a strange feeling that she was floating around the room. Another storm must be shaking the cabin, she thought sleepily, and the singing sound must be the wind. How pleasant it was . . .

The next time Kate woke up, someone was holding her head away from the pillow. She felt the touch of a wooden spoon on her lips and something warm trickling down her throat. She swallowed again and again. Then she opened her eyes.

An Indian woman was standing over her. She brought the spoon to Kate's lips again, but Kate panicked, pushed it away, and struggled to get out of bed. Where were the boys? Then she heard their voices, and in an instant both of their faces were close to her own. She sank back wearily onto the pillow.

"Are you better now, Kate?" Ryan asked.

"Are you all right? What's happened?" Kate managed to whisper.

"We're fine," Alex said. "We've had lots to eat since they came."

"And Bobcat's fine, too," Ryan said gravely. "But we won't let him out until he's all healed. He still limps on one leg."

"Your sister also must eat to get strong," the woman said.

Kate stared at her, afraid. The woman pushed another thick feather pillow under Kate's head. Her brown eyes were warm. Her straight, black hair flowed down her back, shining as Kate's had not for many months. She brought the large wooden spoon to Kate's mouth again. This time the food tasted stronger, like a kind of gruel. Kate did not like the flavour and she did not trust this woman, but she swallowed anyway. She wanted to grow strong. The boys needed her. She managed a few spoonfuls before sleep overwhelmed her again.

The third time Kate woke up, she was still propped up on the pillows and could see Ryan sitting on the foot of her bed, petting Bobcat. The cat was curled up into his perfect oval sleeping position, his wounded leg sticking out only a little.

"Ryan, where's Alex? Where's the woman who was here?"

"Outside. But they'll be back soon. I'm in charge of you," Ryan spoke proudly.

Kate tried to sit up. Ryan grabbed his own pillow and

pushed it beside her. She leaned on it and gradually pulled herself over to the side of the bed. As she sat up, letting her feet hang over the edge of the bed, the room spun before her eyes. It took a minute before it straightened out.

"Now you must tell me what has happened," Kate said.

"Well, these men came and brought us food," Ryan said. "But you were sick and couldn't talk to them."

"Men? What men?"

"Indian men. And a woman — Gajijáwi!" Ryan struggled to say the name correctly.

"Who?"

"Ga-jee-já-wee . . . !"

"When did *she* come?"

"She was here when we woke up. We could smell the cornmeal cakes cooking. Did they smell good!"

"Where was I?" Kate asked. She was beginning to remember her strange dreams and the knocking at the door. She wished she didn't have to ask so many questions. The spinning in her head had subsided, but she felt sick. Her legs and feet began to tingle painfully as the feeling came back to them.

"In your bed, asleep. We tried to wake you up, but we couldn't. Gajijáwi told us that you were very sick and she'd stay and take care of you until you got better. The men left, and when they came back they had more cornmeal and some deer meat. And Gajijáwi crushed up some stuff to make medicine for you. She kept giving you spoonfuls of it."

"How long have I been sick?" asked Kate. She tried putting her feet on the floor, but they tingled so painfully that she drew them up again.

"I don't know," Ryan frowned, trying hard. "A week?"

"A *week*!" A week at the mercy of Indians! She squeezed Ryan's hand. "You must have been worried!"

"Yes, but Gajijáwi said you'd be better soon. I'm sure glad she was right." He seemed unconcerned about the Indians in their house — his worry had been for her.

Kate put a little weight on her feet again. It didn't hurt as much this time.

"I'll help," Ryan said as he catapulted over the top of the bed to stand up next to his sister. He held out his hand.

Kate took small, painful steps to the chair by the fireplace, leaning on her little brother. He was proudly stretching so he'd be as tall as possible. Kate eased herself into the chair and smiled at Ryan.

"Now, Ryan, I want you to tell me everything you've been doing since . . ."

Before she could finish, the door flew open and in stamped Alex, followed by the woman. What had Ryan called her? Gajijáwi.

"Kate!" Alex shouted, racing across the room and throwing himself on her lap. Kate winced, but hugged him for a moment. He felt sturdier already. Then she stared back at the woman by the door — the door!

Was I dreaming that the roof caved in over the door? Kate thought.

"My brothers repaired the roof," the woman said in a low voice. "You were not dreaming."

"We have a big surprise for you, Kate," Alex was saying, but Kate was still staring at the Indian woman, more fearful than before. Had she read Kate's thoughts?

"Are you feeling better?" the woman asked. Her English was very clear.

"Yes," answered Kate shortly. Then, ashamed, she added, "Thank you." Indian or not, this woman had saved her — and the boys. "How did you know we were here?"

"Your father . . ."

"Father!" Kate trembled and gripped the arms of the captain's chair. "Is he alive? You've seen him?"

"Yes. He had a fever and could not speak to us. When he was better, he told us about you, and then we came."

"How is he now?"

"He is . . . improving. He was badly hurt but is gaining his strength now. We will bring him home when he can use his leg again."

Use his leg! thought Kate. "He was hurt? Where? What happened?"

"The men were out hunting when they saw a trail of blood in the snow along the shore of Hay Bay. They found him there in a small canvas tent. He had fallen over the cliff farther west and hit the ice on the water's edge, where he broke his leg. He had crawled along the shore trying to find a place to climb up again, but he couldn't do it."

"How bad was he hurt?"

"His leg was broken in two places, and he also had a flesh wound where a sharp stone cut him deeply. If he had not built a shelter for himself, he would have perished."

Kate shook her head slowly, trying to take it in. She had worried for so long. She had not been wrong when she had imagined Father lying wounded somewhere in the bush.

"When did you find him?"

"Almost a month past, but he was raving with the fever until a week ago. Then he told us about you. We came at once."

Kate felt suddenly exhausted. She got up to go back to her bed and staggered a little. The woman reached out, but it was Alex's shoulder Kate leaned on as she moved the few steps to her bed.

"We've got the best surprise ever for you, Kate," said Alex. Ryan, right beside him, nodded his head.

Kate sank back into the soft feather pillows and stared up at her brothers. Their eyes were sparkling with merriment, and their ruddy cheeks made them look almost healthy. It was obvious they had been outside in the early April sun and winds. She could hardly believe they looked so much better after such a short time. A powerful feeling swept over Kate, and her eyes and nose burnt with tears.

Their ordeal was over and her brothers were just fine. In fact, this whole family would be all right — even Father. As she closed her eyes, she thought of him. He had nearly died in the snow. But now he was safe, and he'd be home soon.

"Kate, you'll never guess our surprise," Alex said.

Kate did not reply. She had fallen into a deep sleep.

CHAPTER
SEVENTEEN

"Kate! Aren't you ever going to get up?" Alex was pulling at Kate's quilts. It was early morning.

"Shhh. You'll wake up Ryan," she whispered. "And where's that woman?"

Alex pointed over to their father's bed. She was stretched out there, sleeping under her own blanket. But even as Kate stared at her, she opened her eyes and sat up. She was fully clothed in a long doeskin tunic and skirt. She slipped on her thick moccasins and moved over to the bed, smiling at Kate and Alex.

"You must be hungry. I'll prepare food," she said. She stepped over to the fireplace, raked the ashes to life, and added two maple sticks. Then she went to the cupboard, took out some cornmeal, and poured it into a bowl. Her quick, sure movements told Kate that the Indian woman was quite at home in their small cabin. It gave Kate an odd feeling.

Alex was pulling on the sleeve of Kate's nightclothes. "Kate, I've got something good for you. Just look!" She watched him fly over to the bucket beside the door and plunk the dipper into it. He lifted it out and carried it over to his sister, dripping liquid all the way. "Try this, Kate," he said.

"No, Alex!" shouted Ryan, who had suddenly come to life. "She can drink the snow water. You'll spoil our surprise."

Alex stopped in his tracks. "Ooops!" he said and headed back to the pail with the dipper.

Her eyes on the Indian woman, Kate sat up and swung her legs over the side of the bed. It was easier today than it had been the day before. On the chair beside her, she saw a clean, neatly mended petticoat and a beautiful new one made of deerskin, just like Sarah's. She slipped into them slowly. It felt strange to get dressed after being in bed so long. The deerskin petticoat was heavy, but warm.

The Indian woman was leaning over the fireplace and flipping cornmeal cakes in the iron spider frying pan. Kate sniffed the aroma as she took her place at the table. She ate small bites of the cornmeal cakes and they tasted good. The boys, still in their nightshirts, ate greedily.

"Thank you . . . Gajijáwi," said Kate after she had eaten.

The woman smiled at her. "My name means 'gives flowers' in your language," she said simply. "Are you feeling better?"

"Yes, much stronger today." Kate paused. She felt as if she had forgotten how to have a conversation with any-one, much less with an Indian woman. "Do you live in these parts?" she finally asked.

"Yes. My family lives in Tyendinaga. But we came here from New York State."

"Oh!" said Kate. "We used to live in Albany! Did you live there?" Immediately she felt foolish. She had never seen Indians in Albany. But Gajijáwi smiled.

"No, we lived farther north, in the Mohawk Valley."

"Are you Loyalists, then?" asked Kate doubtfully.

"Yes," said Gajijáwi proudly. "My people fought many battles for the British. After our farms were burnt by the revolutionaries, we came to Canada. We were given land along the Grand River and also to the northwest of here — on the Bay of Quinte. We have been living there for four years now."

"So is that where Father is, with the — with your people?"

"Yes, he asks my brothers about you all the time. They may bring him home soon on a toboggan."

"Good," Kate said. But she wasn't sure she meant it. She was glad that Father was well, but she would have to be up and working when he returned. She still felt as though she were stuck to her chair with tiredness. And though this Mohawk woman was kind, who knew what her brothers would be like?

Gajijáwi was looking closely at Kate's troubled face. "Don't worry," she said quietly. "My brother Tówi has gone to the home of your friends, the Shaws, to see if someone can come to help you. Your father told us about them."

Suddenly, Kate's heart leapt with joy. Would Sarah come? Then Sarah's words came back to Kate: "You've no reason to fear any Indians around here." Perhaps Sarah was right.

Gajijáwi was still watching Kate closely. "I will come each day and help until someone else comes to help you."

A silence fell heavy between them.

Then Kate nodded at Gajijáwi. She knew she would need help for a while.

The boys had left the table during Kate's conversation with Gajijáwi, but now they returned and were standing one on each side of her, dressed and ready to go out.

"You're getting to be big boys, dressing all by yourselves." Kate smiled proudly at her brothers.

"Of course," Alex said, and went over to the door. "Gajijáwi, we're going out to play now."

"No, Alex, you can't go out alone," Kate said.

"We can so," retorted Alex, already opening the door. Gajijáwi laid her hand on Kate's arm. "It's all right, Kate. My other brother is working nearby and will watch the boys. I'll take them there."

"Oh!" Kate said. A lot seemed to have happened during the week she was ill. The boys had certainly taken to these strangers. "I'll go, too." She got up suddenly and pulled away from Gajijáwi's touch. But she had to stand still as the room spun around her. She knew she was too weak to go. She slowly walked over to the window, leaned against the sill, and watched them leave through the patched door.

Through the window Kate saw Gajijáwi disappear into the woods with the boys. So often she had wished for someone else to take charge of the boys for a while. Now it was happening and she felt strange, afraid and almost sad. When Gajijáwi reemerged from the woods, Kate was still standing there, staring. Kate hurried over to her father's chair and sat down. She did not want Gajijáwi to know she had been watching.

"My brothers are working in your woods," Gajijáwi explained as she brushed snow from her skirt. "Alex and Ryan are planning a surprise especially for you, and they are eager to work on it. I promised not to tell you what they are doing."

"Oh, I'm not worried," Kate said quickly. How was it that Gajijáwi always seemed to know what she was thinking? "The boys are looking quite well . . . and happy." She must not let the Mohawk woman know that she was afraid.

"Yes, they grew stronger much faster than you did. But I suspect that you went without food longer." Gajijáwi reached out and touched Kate's face. Startled, Kate looked up and met her eyes. "You have been very brave, Kate," she said quietly.

There was a loud stamping of feet at the door. Kate tightened her hands on the sides of her father's chair. The door burst open and Kate saw a tall dark-skinned man and the small bent figure of a woman in a deep brown cape and a brown woollen scarf wound round and round her head.

As she unwrapped the shawl, Kate saw the wrinkled, smiling face of Grandma Shaw. She held out her arms to Kate. "Kate, my dear. You poor, poor child."

Kate flew the few steps across the floor and clung to the old woman.

Grandma Shaw patted Kate's back.

"Look what Tówi has for us!" she said.

The Indian man pulled a huge package from his bag. "There is more," he said to Gajijáwi. "Our brother found a buck yesterday. He took it to the village. Our supplies are scarce, too, but we can spare these."

Gajijáwi unwrapped the dry skins around the package and eagerly peeked in. "Fresh meat! That's what Kate needs!" She hurried over to the cupboard.

Grandma Shaw clasped the man's hand warmly. "Thank you, Tówi, for the meat and for coming to fetch me."

"You are welcome," said the man. He nodded to his sister and was gone.

Grandma Shaw took off her cloak, shawls, and scarves and put on an apron she took from her small carpetbag, then settled in a chair to warm herself by the fire. She talked all the while. "Oh, Kate, we were so sorry to hear about your problems. I told my Will that your father shouldn't be going out alone into this uninhabited area with three children. But Will said he wasn't going to interfere in another man's business."

Kate was overwhelmed. Her ordeal was over and Grandma Shaw was here, a grandma just like her own grandma. It was wonderful! So why did she feel like crying? She sniffed back her tears. She must not cry.

"Here, come and sit beside me," said Grandma Shaw. Kate came and sat at Grandma Shaw's feet, and they both relaxed in the warm glow of the fire. "You know, it wasn't easy for anyone this winter," Grandma Shaw continued. "Wild animals perished in the storms, and fish swam to deeper waters because it froze so deeply near shore. Everyone was hungry and a few starved to death. We even had to kill our cow and eat her."

Kate's tears started to fall and flowed down her cheeks in an unending stream. What was she crying for? The cow? Her tears were even dripping onto the floor in front of her. It didn't make any sense, but she just couldn't stop. She bent her head over and hoped Grandma Shaw wouldn't see. She was glad Father was not here just now. She knew what he would say! She tried to stop and her throat seemed to tighten and make a gurgling sound.

The older woman just sat there staring into the warm red flames of the fireplace and placed a small, wrinkled, firm hand on Kate's shoulder. "Tears are nothing to be ashamed of at all," she said.

Through her tears, Kate saw Gajijáwi take her coat and slip outside. The door closed, and Kate broke out into loud sobs. "I was so afraid," she said between clenched teeth and body-wracking sobs. "I thought we would all . . . die! . . . I was afraid I would die first and there would be no one to take care of the boys. In fact, I was already too weak to . . ." The sobs were easing up but she stopped to catch her breath.

"You were very brave," said Grandma Shaw. "It's a marvel how you kept going. And thank the mercy of God that He sent the Mohawks to rescue you."

Kate took a deep breath and let it out slowly. She felt much better, as if the tears had washed away every bit of her weeks of worry and fear. "We prayed every day —

especially Ryan. He was sure that help would come. I never thought that God would send the Mohawks."

"They were better prepared than the rest of us. Last fall, they seemed to notice signs in nature that pointed to this bad winter. We knew it would be a hard one, but we had no idea how hard. But they did! And they helped many white people to survive. They know which herbs and roots are safe to eat, and we do not. One of our neighbour families died from eating poisonous roots a week ago."

"We wouldn't have made it if it hadn't been for Bobcat," Kate said. As though he'd heard his name, Bobcat strolled over to Kate and rubbed against her ankles, purring.

"Bobcat!" said Grandma Shaw, staring at the cat. "I do declare that's our Bobcat!"

"Yes, I'm sure he is. He showed up here in the winter, I think he stowed away on your wagon when Sarah and her father came up last fall. He stayed in the wild until he got caught in the storms. Then he came to live with us."

Grandma Shaw reached over and stroked the cat.

"We had only a little sugar to put in water when Bobcat started hunting for us. For two whole weeks, he brought us a rabbit every day — and he would have kept going if he hadn't got hurt!"

"God works in wondrous ways," Grandma Shaw mumbled almost to herself. Then she said loudly, "Bobcat's a great hunter, for even rabbits were scarce this winter."

Kate sat looking at the flames dancing in the fireplace. It had been a long time since she had had a chance to sit and look into the fire without cares — back when her mother was alive.

She could hear Father saying, "You're going to spoil Kate, letting her play all the time."

But Mother had just smiled and said, "Oh, Kate will be grown before we know it. Just let her be." So Kate had played until Mother died and Grandma came. Sometimes she had worked hard for Grandma, but after she died, too, Kate had had to work all the time.

Kate suddenly felt guilty. She wiped her eyes, got up, and stepped over to the table. "I should see what I can do to prepare supper."

Grandma Shaw jumped up from her chair. "My dear child, you sit right down. I'm going to do that. Let's see now what our friend Gajijáwi has left here."

Kate sank back into Father's big chair.

CHAPTER
EIGHTEEN

"Ah," said Grandma Shaw. "A fresh roast of venison —
all washed and in the iron pot. I'll put this over our fire."
After hanging the pot, she hurried over to her bag and
dug down into it. She rummaged around a little and
pulled out a small piece of paper and handed it to Kate.
Kate opened up the paper.

April 3/1788

Dear Kate,

*I'm writing this awful fast. Grandma is packing to go
to help you. I want to go but Ma won't let me. She says
I'll have to help her now Grandma is going.*

*It was a terrible winter here, too. We almost ran out
of food. We had to kill the cow and eat her. But I must
say no more. Ma says to be cheerful because you have
troubles of your own. I am so glad you are all right!
Many folks here are still hungry. A few supplies have
come up from Adolphustown, so it should start being a
little better.*

*What does it feel like to be a heroine? Tówi says you
were very brave.*

Your best friend,
Sarah

Grandma Shaw was bustling around the kitchen,
taking parcels out of her bag, and opening the cupboard
to put them inside. "I'll just put these things here for
the moment, though I know they'll be rearranged
later. A woman likes to order her own kitchen, eh, Kate?
When you're feeling better, you can take a look."

"Oh — no, that's all right," said Kate, startled. She
had thought Grandma Shaw meant that Gajijáwi would
rearrange things. "It's nice to have a grandma . . . I don't
mean to say that you're my . . . I mean, I've wished that
. . ." She stopped, confused.

"Of course, you'd like your own grandma. I understand, Kate, and it's all right. But since she can't be here,
I'll try to be a grandma in her place. You could even call
me Grandma if you wish. I know I can never be your real
grandma, but . . ."

"That would be just fine, Grandma," Kate said with
a little smile. She watched Grandma Shaw stirring
together things in the big mixing bowl. It felt good not
to worry about what would be for supper. Anything
would taste wonderful.

"Why don't you write a letter to Sarah?" Grandma
Shaw suggested.

"I would love to, but I have no paper. Besides, when
could I send it to her?"

"Oh, one of these days, Tówi will be going back to Adolphustown for supplies, and he would take your letter if it was ready."

"Do you know the Mohawks very well?" Kate asked.

"Oh, yes, quite a lot of them. We've known Gajijáwi and her brothers since we first arrived."

"Can we . . . trust them?" Kate had to know for sure. "I worry about Ryan and Alex. Are they safe with them?"

"Very safe. The Mohawks have adjusted better than the white people to this area, though they've been here no longer. They know the bush in a way we do not, but this winter has been hard for them, too."

This wasn't the answer Kate was looking for — Grandma Shaw had misunderstood her question. Suddenly Kate was ashamed of her lingering fears. She of all people should believe that the Mohawks were her friends.

Just then there was a great stomping on the front doorstep. The door pushed open and in tumbled Alex and Ryan, followed by Gajijáwi.

The rosy-cheeked boys rushed over to Kate at the same time — tracking snow and mud across the floor. "I hope you're soon well enough for our surprise," said Alex. Ryan was giving Kate his mysterious grin.

"Look at those tracks!" Kate scolded gently.

"Maybe tomorrow she'll be ready," said Gajijáwi. "Don't rush your sister."

For the first time, Kate smiled up at Gajijáwi with no doubt in her eyes.

◈

"I'm going to make a new batch of bread," said Grandma Shaw to Kate the very next morning. She was washing the breakfast dishes and Kate was drying.

"I can help," said Kate. "I do feel stronger today."

"I'm sure you can, but maybe you'd like to go for a walk. The fresh air would do you good — maybe put some colour back in those cheeks."

"I'd like that," Kate said quietly, "but I might get lost."

Just then Gajijáwi stepped through the door. She had already taken the boys to help her brothers. "You won't get lost with me," she said. "We wouldn't need to go far. And it is a lovely day."

Kate was starting to enjoy the company of her new friend. It was great to have all this help and company. She untied her apron and reached for her outdoor clothes.

Wrapped up snugly in her cloak, Kate and Gajijáwi stepped out onto the frozen ground in front of the cabin. The banks of snow had melted to a quarter of their previous height. Little ice patches had formed on the ground where the snow had melted during the day and frozen again at night.

It is spring, Kate thought. Back home near Albany, spring would have arrived almost a month ago. But even here, it was finally coming. Kate and Gajijáwi entered the woods and walked along the pathway towards Kate's special place.

Kate looked around cautiously and asked, "Are you sure there aren't any bears nearby?"

"Yes, I'm sure. We would have seen them. Alex showed me your special house. He said you brought your friend Sarah there."

Kate smiled as she thought of Sarah. "Now that it's spring, the rest of the Shaws might come to visit again and bring Sarah."

"I'm sure they will," said Gajijáwi. "But it's been a terribly hard winter. Don't be disappointed if they can't come for a while. In the meantime, my brother Tówi may be going down to Adolphustown in a few days. Why don't you write your friend a letter for him to take along?"

"I'd like to, but I haven't any paper to write on. I'd have to tear a page out of our Bible, and I don't want to do that."

Gajijáwi lead Kate a little way into the forest and paused at a tall white birch tree. "I'll get a piece of bark for you," she said.

"Gajijáwi, do you live with your brothers?" Kate asked as she watched her friend peel a beige-white strip from the bark.

"Yes, I do now," Gajijáwi said. Kate thought she heard a catch in Gajijáwi's voice. "My parents died during the war. I lived with an aunt and uncle until the war was over and we all came to Canada. My uncle and aunt settled at Grand River, but my brothers wanted to come here. I chose to come with them."

"Oh." Kate was silent, then she burst out, "Do you miss your mother sometimes?" She looked down so that Gajijáwi could not see her eyes.

"My brothers are glad to have me build their fires and cook their meals. But I still miss my mother, and I think I always will."

They walked on for a while in silence, then Kate said in a low voice, "I miss my mother a lot."

"Tell me about her. Then I'll tell you about my mother."

"Well, she was . . . beautiful. Not like me at all — she had blond hair, like the boys, only very long. Longer than yours, even," said Kate shyly. "She used to let me brush it for her. And she was . . . very happy. She was always singing and laughing. She even used to make Father laugh."

"I can see that."

"You can?" Kate looked up at Gajijáwi with happy, shining eyes.

"Yes. You're smiling now, just remembering all those good times."

Kate realized this was the first time she had been able to talk about her mother without holding back tears. In fact, she hadn't even felt like crying.

"Your father must miss her very much, too," Gajijáwi said.

"Father?" Kate stopped for a moment. "Oh, yes, I suppose. But he can't miss her as much as I do." Kate couldn't keep the bitterness from her voice. "He never speaks of her. He gave away all her things. Grandma kept her shawl for me, but I don't dare wear it for fear he'd get rid of that, too. It's all I have to remind me of my mother. Any time I mention her, Father gets cross and starts to scold me about something or other —"

Suddenly a memory came to Kate, something she had forgotten until now. Once, when she was very small, some men had come to dig a new well on their farm in Albany. Father had warned Kate to stay away from the hole, but it had been such fun to watch the dirt being brought up on the winch, bucketful by bucketful. Later that day, she had spent a whole afternoon watching new-born kittens until she fell asleep in the hay.

It was evening when she woke. The farm was strangely silent, and when she emerged, blinking, from the barn, she saw her parents huddled together by the new well. She ran to them.

"Mother, I'm hungry," she had said, tugging at her mother's skirt to get her attention.

Her parents had stared at her for a moment, then her father roared, "Where have you been?"

Startled, Kate burst into tears and sobbed while Father scolded her loudly and Mother hugged her so hard it hurt. Much later, when Mother came to tuck her into bed, Kate asked tearfully, "Is Father still angry?"

"He wasn't really angry," Mother had said, stroking her hair. "He thought you had fallen into the well, and blamed himself for not keeping a cover on it — and then he was so happy to see you standing there all safe and sound . . ." Mother had seemed to be searching for a way to explain. "It's all those feelings mixed together that made your father speak to you the way he did."

Remembering, Kate turned to Gajijáwi and said, "Perhaps he does miss her. Grown-ups are funny about things like that." She shook her head. "Now tell me about your mother, Gajijáwi."

"She was known as 'Walks the Fire' — that's the translation in your language. She earned that name because, when she was still a young girl, she saved a small child from a burning wigwam."

"That was very brave."

"There are different kinds of courage, Kate. Her brave act was truly brave, but it was over in a short time. She told me once that she hardly realized what she was doing until it was all over." Gajijáwi paused, then said thoughtfully, "It takes another, harder kind of courage to act bravely day after day as you did this winter."

"I did what I had to do," said Kate, and she was suddenly very tired. "I think I'd like to go back now."

Gajijáwi took her hand and together they walked slowly back to the cabin.

CHAPTER
NINETEEN

April 9, 1788

Dear Sarah,

I'm writing this letter now, so it'll be ready in time when someone goes down to Adolphustown for supplies. It'll probably reach you in the hand of Gajijáwi's brother, Túwi.

You'll never believe this, but Bobcat is here! He must have been hiding in your wagon when you came in November, and then got left behind. He turned up one night in February, meowing on our stoop. And he saved us from starving! I'll tell you more about it when I see you. He's a wonderful cat.

Gajijáwi stayed with us until your grandma came, and Gajijáwi still comes back in the daytime to help us. Grandma Shaw is wonderful, just like my own grandma was. Maybe she's even a little bit kinder and doesn't let me do much work. I think that's because I was so sick. Gajijáwi is wonderful, too. She gave me this birchbark to write on. Doesn't it make wonderful paper?

Alex and Ryan are just fine, and Bobcat's leg is

getting better. Did I tell you he broke his leg? I'm running out of space so I will stop now. I hope this letter finds you and your family in good health.

Ever your best friend,

Kate

P.S. I guess Tówi told you all about Father.

"Kate, c'mon!" Alex said. "Hurry up and finish writing that letter. Gajijáwi says you're strong enough now to see our surprise!"

Ryan smiled mysteriously. "You'll sure like it."

Four days had passed since Grandma Shaw had come to stay with Kate and the boys. Gajijáwi stayed with her own two brothers in a small shelter set up in the middle of their woods, but she came to their cabin every day to visit and to help Grandma Shaw. Kate had been feeling much stronger since her first walk with Gajijáwi. The boys' eagerness to go outside infected her, and she hurried as she signed her name to her letter.

Alex brought Kate's cloak and woollen hat and mitts. She pulled them on while Gajijáwi helped the boys into their red and blue cloaks. Then Gajijáwi threw on her own hooded raccoon cloak and opened the door.

Kate stepped out into the still morning. The sun was shining brightly and the air was warm. Gajijáwi led the way and Alex followed in her steps. Ryan walked behind him but kept turning back to Kate. They had to go carefully. The path through the clearing was covered with a layer of melted snow, and was very slippery.

Once in the forest, Alex pushed past Gajijáwi and

began to run ahead.

"Wait," Kate shouted, and Gajijáwi turned to her.

"Alex will not get lost," she said, "but to ease your mind, I'll follow him. Ryan can show you the way." She disappeared around a bend in the trail.

Kate looked fearfully into the shadows beside the trail. It was still a bit dark. Scampering sounds came from all sides. She didn't feel as safe as she had when Gajijáwi was in sight. She looked down at Ryan doubtfully, and he took her hand.

"Don't worry, Kate," he beamed up at her. "I can follow the trail. Gajijáwi showed us how to remember. There are landmarks all along."

"Like what?"

"Oh . . . this stone over here. Isn't it a funny shape? And that tree ahead, with the sticking-out branch — it's pointing out the way to go."

They had walked perhaps twenty minutes when Kate noticed it was much lighter. Trees here and there along the path had troughs of bark stuck into hatchet slashes in their trunks. Birchbark baskets hanging below were catching the steady drips of liquid. Kate knew what was ahead; but for the boys' sake, she acted surprised when she and Ryan entered the maple grove.

She and Sarah had passed through this spot last fall. Today the sun shone down and lit up the whole area, for there were no leaves at all to hide its rays. The trees hadn't even started to bud out yet. Kate, looking in all directions, saw tree trunks with hatchet slashes.

"Come on, Kate!" Alex shouted. Impatient as always,

he had come racing back along the path to find Kate and hurry her along. Ryan dropped Kate's hand and ran between the trees towards him as fast as his short legs would carry him. Kate smiled and stepped up her pace. Soon the path broke into a clearing.

"Look, Kate!" cried Alex and Ryan.

A big fire burnt briskly in the clearing's centre. Over the fire hung seven huge iron kettles. Gajijáwi was standing near the fire, talking to two men whose backs were turned to Kate. They were dressed in skins like the ones Gajijáwi wore. One of them was bent over, stoking the fire. The other man dipped a wooden paddle into the nearest kettle and looked carefully at the sap he had drawn out.

Kate's face broke into a smile. "Maple syrup!"

"That's not all," said Alex. He was almost too excited to talk. "Gajijáwi's brothers have a potful that they've been boiling and boiling. Desagósnye says it's ready." He beckoned importantly, and ran towards Gajijáwi.

"She's here!" Alex shouted in a shrill voice. "Are you ready?" Gajijáwi and her brothers turned and grinned at the boy, who was waving both arms in the air.

The man that Kate had seen testing the contents of one of the kettles now lifted it off the long spit and carried it a few yards away.

"That's Desagósnye," said Ryan. "And that's Tówi." He pointed to the taller man, who was carrying an empty pot towards the highest snowbank in the clearing. He set the pot down, filled it with snow, and pushed hard to pack it in. Then he came back and set the pot down in front of Kate. The snow inside sparkled clean and white. Desagósnye followed and set his hot kettle down with a hiss of steam.

"Watch," said Alex. He plunged a dipper into the kettle of hot syrup and poured the contents onto the clean snow in thick puddles. The boys stood spellbound with delight as the liquid hardened before their eyes. Then Alex grabbed the end of one of the golden-brown puddles and tossed it towards Kate. As she caught it, the soft substance pulled down from her hand.

"It's the best candy ever," said Ryan.

Kate flipped her wrist and the maple taffy rolled around her fingers. She raised it to her mouth and took a big, sticky bite. It was the best maple taffy she had ever tasted.

◇

For the next few days, Kate spent her time going to the maple grove with the others while Grandma Shaw kept up the work in the cabin, preparing meals, and tidying the place. Kate offered to help stir the kettles, but Gajijáwi refused.

"No, Kate," she said. "You are still recovering. You did enough work for a mother and a father combined. And you were as brave as a hunter. Now you can be a young girl again."

So Kate played with her brothers and walked in the fresh air and sunshine. In the evenings, after the boys had gone to bed, she and Grandma Shaw talked and worked by the firelight. Grandma Shaw was knitting a new short-coat for Sarah's little brother, and Kate was making herself a pair of moccasins, just like Gajijáwi had. Her Mohawk friend had brought all the materials and shown her how to make them herself.

One morning, Desagósnye was stirring the syrup kettles alone when Kate and the others arrived. Kate wondered where Tówi had gone, but her friends did not answer her questions so she knew it was to be a surprise and she did not want to spoil their fun. Perhaps she would be getting another letter from Sarah. That evening after supper there was a knock on the door, and when Grandma Shaw opened it, Kate could see Tówi standing there. He handed Grandma Shaw a large round basket.

Kate could see a roll of birchbark peeking out of a corner of the full basket. Grandma Shaw saw Kate's hopeful face and handed her the scroll.

"Yes, Kate, I've been to Adolphustown and back," Tówi said. "I have brought you a letter from Sarah. And another surprise will be coming soon."

But Kate was only interested in her letter. She opened the scroll carefully so as not to crack the birchbark. Even Sarah did not have any paper to spare, she saw.

April 15, 1788

Dear Kate,

I was very excited to hear from you. And to hear about Bobcat was absolutely marvelous. I always knew he was a great cat. But Ma doesn't believe he could have saved you from starving, so you will have to tell us all the story.

   Many folks here are still hungry, but a few supplies have come up from King's Town. That will help make matters better.

   Gajijáwi sounds like a nice friend but please remember I'm your very best friend and I'm coming to see you just as soon as Pa has time free.

                    Your very best friend,
                    Sarah

P.S. Say Hello to Grandma for me. I'm glad to share my grandma with you, but tell her we miss her.

P.S.S. I made you a lovely pair of mitts. I'll bring them when I come. You'll have them for next winter.

❖

Several days later, the second surprise arrived. The cabin door opened silently and three tall figures stood there.

"Father! Father!" the boys shouted.

Kate looked up from the floor she was sweeping. It really was Father this time, standing in the early evening light of the open doorway, leaning on Gajijáwi's brothers. He was thin and pale, but he was alive and he was back home. Kate could hardly believe it.

"Ryan, Alex," Father said quietly as he started to limp forward. Still leaning on Tówi, he held out an arm. The twins ran straight at him and nearly knocked him over. But Father didn't seem to mind. His head bowed, he held them tightly, one boy at a time.

Kate stood back a little, beside Gajijáwi. Bobcat took one cowering look at the newcomer and slunk under

Kate's bed, dragging his lame leg behind him. Father looked up at last.

"Kate," he said. His voice seemed hoarse. "You — you're looking well."

"Gajijáwı and Grandma Shaw have taken good care of us," Kate said stiffly.

"You have a very brave daughter," Grandma Shaw said to Father. "She cared for your sons like a real mother."

"Yes, I know," Father said. He took his daughter's thin hand in his. "It's a wonder how you ever managed when I was gone. You took good care of the boys, Kate, and I'm grateful. I thought you'd all be . . ." He choked a little and did not finish his sentence.

"I — I'm glad you're back," said Kate shyly. Father seemed to have changed, she thought. He was kinder and his voice was softer — not really like himself at all. Still, she hoped Grandma Shaw and Gajijáwi would not leave yet.

Father cleared his throat with a dry cough. "Thank God it's over." He turned to Gajijáwi with his hand outstretched. "I guess you'll be going now."

"Kate is still weak," Gajijáwi said quietly, "so I'll stay and help Grandma until Kate is stronger. I'll go tonight with my brothers to our shelter in the maple bush, but I'll be back in the morning, as usual."

Father nodded. "I am grateful for all your help. But I hope that we'll soon be able to manage. Grandma Shaw, they must miss you back home, too."

"I'm sure they do, but not as much as this poor child needs me," said Grandma Shaw sharply as she put her hand on Kate's shoulder. Kate saw Father's face grow a little pale. She had a strange feeling that Grandma Shaw didn't like Father very much.

"Now I'll prepare food," said Gajijáwi. She looked at her brothers, who hesitated.

"Come in, come in," said Father. He motioned his friends over to the fireside and offered his chair to Desagósnye.

Kate dragged the low bench from the side of the table and set it down for Father and Tówi. The twins sat there, too, on either side of Father. They might as well have been glued to his sides.

Kate hurried over to the cupboard to set the table while Gajijáwi pulled out the iron spider pan and dropped the cornmeal batter into it. Grandma Shaw was slicing bread and placing other foods on the table.

"I'll keep them from burning," Kate said. Gajijáwi handed her the frying pan. With a very large wooden scoop, Kate watched the yellow cakes bubble and sizzle.

She glanced over at the table. Father was laughing with Desagósnye and Tówi, and he was hugging Ryan and tousling Alex's hair. Not once did he even glance at her.

For the first time in days, Kate felt a knot in her stomach. She turned back to the fire.

CHAPTER
TWENTY

When Gajijáwi arrived at seven the next morning, the family had already finished eating and Kate was washing up the dishes.

"Good morning," Father said. "I believe it's going to be another fine day for syrup. There's nothing like these mild days and cold nights for a good sap run." He was pulling Alex's cloak on over the boy's head. Alex beamed up at his father.

Gajijáwi smiled at him and hung up her cloak. She hurried over to Kate, grabbed the towel, and started drying the dishes.

"The boys and I, we're heading out for the sugar bush," Father went on. "I'm afraid I'll not be much help with this game leg, but it'll be fun to watch. And the boys want to pull more taffy," he laughed.

"Yes, the sweet water will run fast today," Gajijáwi said.

"Kate, where are those thorns for the boys' cloaks?" asked Father. Ryan's cloak gaped open at the neck, and Father was fumbling around the cloth, looking for the hawthorn needle.

"It must have dropped out," Kate said. She stepped over beside the boys and ran her hand along the floor by the door. She found it right next to Father's foot.

"Thanks, Kate," Father said. "Well, we'll be off." He turned to follow the boys, who had dashed out ahead.

Bobcat emerged from under Kate's bed. Since Father's return, he'd been lying low. But he was in the habit of accompanying the boys to the sugar bush every day and wasn't about to change his routine just because Father was home. Besides, he needed to get out.

Kate held her breath, but Father was watching the boys and didn't notice Bobcat slipping through the door just after him.

About an hour later, Father returned without the boys. He burst into the cabin and banged the door shut behind him. His face was drawn into a tight grimace of pain. Kate hurried over to help him with his cloak.

"Nothing wrong with his arms, Kate," said Grandma Shaw from her rocking chair. Father looked up at her in surprise.

A silence hung heavy in the room.

Kate asked, "Where are the boys?"

"Back at the sugar bush," answered Father shortly. He collapsed into his chair with a groan. "You can fetch them later if you're worried. So stop your fussing over them, Kate. Now help me with my boots!"

A grumpy *humph* came from Grandma Shaw's corner. Kate and her father both looked in her direction. But she was staring down and her lightning fingers never stopped their busy knitting.

Silently Kate unlaced Father's boots and set a stool under his leg. The tight lines on Father's face eased a little, and he said gruffly, "Thank you, Kate. This leg . . ."

Kate nodded and went back to her chore of grinding wheat into flour. They were having fresh bread for the midday meal, a special treat. Father didn't say anything more, and when Kate glanced at him a while later, he had dozed off.

They had to wake him for the noon meal. "It's better," he said. "I could get up." He started to rise but sat back, obviously in pain. Kate served him his food at his chair.

"Would you let me look at it, Mr. O'Carr?" Gajijáwi asked after the meal was over. "I have ointments made from herbs. They will help to draw out the soreness."

"If it's not too much trouble," said Father stiffly.

"It's no trouble. I'll wash the wound, too." Gajijáwi poured hot water into a pan. She took a handful of herbs from a small leather bag, dropped it into the water, and stirred gently. She got some cloth from the cupboard, came over, and knelt beside Father to unwrap the dressing on his leg. When she was done, she asked Kate to bring the pan over.

Kate stared over Gajijáwi's shoulder and winced at the sight of Father's jagged, red wound. Father sat rigidly still as Gajijáwi bathed it gently, dried it, and applied some ointment. It looked to Kate a little like the Balm of Gilead that Grandma used to make from buds in the spring. Finally Gajijáwi wrapped the leg in clean broadcloth that Kate had pulled out of their trunk. Father gave a relieved sigh as Gajijáwi turned away and threw the water out the door.

When Gajijáwi came back inside, she said, "Mr. O'Carr, your wound will heal faster and better if you stay off it — for a while."

"A while! How long is that?" The sharpness had returned to Father's voice.

"I cannot tell you. The wound has broken open again. Perhaps in another week you can walk on it, but I doubt it. Kate, I'll show you how to make poultices. We should regularly cover that open sore." Father scowled at Gajijáwi, but she seemed not to notice. She went on, "I'll get you a couple of strong sticks and you can whittle them into shape to make two sturdy supports. That way you can move about a little without having to put any weight on that leg. Most of the time, you must keep the leg up. Walking even lightly on it is not wise. You must be cautious!"

"You are treating me like an invalid!"

"If you lose your leg, you will be one," Grandma Shaw said sharply in a raspy voice. "Didn't the good Lord give you any common sense?"

Father looked as though he would explode. But both women and Kate were now staring at him. Gradually his anger subsided, and he lay on his bed.

"Well, I'll make the crutches, anyway," he grumbled.

Kate knew he liked whittling. She was glad Gajijáwi had thought of that. "Let's go out now and look for those sticks," Kate suggested.

Gajijáwi glanced at Kate, then Father, and then back

at Kate with a knowing look. They grabbed their coats and left Grandma Shaw and Father to fume about his helpless condition. As they hurried outside, they could hear the knitting needles clacking. Just off the stoop, Gajijáwi burst out laughing. "Your father is outnumbered by the three of us!"

It was true. For once, it wasn't Kate being over-powered by the twins and Father, it was Father being bossed by Grandma Shaw and Gajijáwi. She started to giggle as they hunted for the sticks.

❖

"Kate! Kate!" The boys were back. Kate hurried to help them off with their cloaks.

"Shhh," she told them. "Father had a bad morning and needs his sleep." He had fallen asleep while Kate and Gajijáwi were out and had not woken up since.

Alex said in a hoarse whisper, "Look, Kate. I brought you some taffy." He handed her a small birchbark basket.

"Thank you, Alex," Kate said quietly. "That looks delicious."

"I brought some, too!" said Ryan.

"I know, and you did a good job. Now let's roll it out on the table."

Kate guided her brothers over to the table, glancing cautiously at Father. He had not even moved.

She rolled out the taffy with both hands, took a knife from the rack above the cupboard, and cut a piece for each of them.

"Only one piece?" Ryan complained.

"You'll spoil your supper if you have more. And besides, I'm sure you had plenty in the bush," answered Kate sternly. Alex and Ryan exchanged guilty looks. "Come to the fire and I'll tell you a story," suggested Kate.

The boys shared Father's chair, and Kate sat beside them on a stool. She looked around the cabin. Bobcat was cleaning himself on her bed. Everything was neat and clean, and Grandma Shaw and Gajijáwi were making supper: dried-venison stew with carrots and turnips. And there would probably be cornmeal biscuits to go on top of it. Kate's stomach growled pleasantly and she sighed with happiness. It was almost like having her own grandma back again. And even though she was older than Kate, Gajijáwi was a good friend.

Kate took a deep breath and began, "Once upon a time . . ."

❖

Father got up to eat, but he was silent and brooding, and supper became a gloomy affair. Everyone ate in silence. When he was like this before, Kate had always scurried about looking for ways to cheer Father, or at least make things easy for him. But today, Kate was annoyed. The afternoon had been so pleasant, and now he had almost ruined the day with his black mood.

After supper was eaten and the dishes were washed, Grandma Shaw began to set out the boys' nightclothes. Gajijáwi was getting ready to go. She was almost out the door when Father said abruptly, "Thank you for all your help, Gajijáwi. I'll be able to pay you for your services when my supplies come up from Adolphustown."

"I need no pay," Gajijáwi replied. "In this new land, we Loyalists all help each other. I have enjoyed my time with Grandma, Kate, and the children. I will be back tomorrow."

"That's not necessary," said Father. "Kate is perfectly capable of managing now. And by the way, when is Tówi going to Adolphustown?"

"I'm not sure. I'll ask him."

"I'm sending Mrs. Shaw back with him," Father said bluntly.

Kate gasped. How could Father be so — so rude? But she didn't dare speak.

Gajijáwi turned and looked at Kate's flushed, angry face. "Kate, is that all right with you?" she asked quietly.

"No, it's not!" Kate answered. She stole a glance at Father, then took a deep breath. "Could Gajijáwi come later in the morning to help me with the washing?"

Father glared at Kate, but before he could protest, Gajijáwi nodded and said, "I'll come." She slipped through the door and closed it behind her.

Father scowled at Kate. "Get the boys ready for bed. They've had a busy day." He looked up only briefly, to kiss each of the boys good-night, then went back to staring into the fire.

Grandma Shaw slipped quietly into Kate's bed, where she had been sleeping since Father's return. It had been a long day for her, too. In no time at all, Kate could hear the boys' heavy breathing from their bed and Grandma Shaw's light snoring.

Kate decided to work on her moccasins. There would be enough light if she worked in the glow of the fire. She opened her trunk to get them and looked for a while at her mother's shawl, folded neatly inside. She took it out, gave it a quick shake, and draped it around her shoulders. It made her feel special, like a lady. Why shouldn't she wear it? It was warm and beautiful, and it shouldn't be wasted. She would tell Father that if he said anything about it.

She thought about how he had acted this evening. When Father had had these bad times before, she had always felt it was *her* fault. In fact, Father had told her it was. But he'd been rude to Grandma Shaw and Gajijáwi, and Kate knew it was *not* their fault. They were wonderful. So maybe Father wasn't always right as she had assumed.

Father shuffled in his chair by the fireplace. "Kate, it's time for my tea," he grumbled. "Have you forgotten?"

Kate came over silently and took the steaming kettle from the hearth. She took it to the cupboard and filled a teapot. Then she scooped out two teaspoonfuls of tea from a little bowl and stirred them into the pot to steep. She lifted the heavy kettle and carried it back to the hearth. If Father had noticed the shawl, he wasn't saying anything about it.

In a few minutes, without lifting his head, Father asked peevishly, "Kate, what's holding you up? That tea should have been ready long ago."

Kate squeezed her lips tightly together but said nothing. Her grandma had always said to let tea steep sufficiently or the true flavour was lost. But she got up and stirred the tea vigorously, then poured out a cupful. Father seemed to think that if he couldn't be active, she should be.

She stepped into the glowing light of the fireside and handed him his tin cup. "Thank you, Kate," he said in a quieter voice.

She answered calmly, "You're welcome."

Then Father suddenly looked at Kate, really looked at her. "That's your *mother's* shawl!" he exclaimed. There was a hint of anger in his tone.

"Yes, it is," said Kate. "Grandma kept it for me."

"Well, put it away!" growled Father.

"Meow!"

Not now, Bobcat, thought Kate in dismay.

"What's that cat doing in here, Kate?" Father hissed. "I told you he wasn't allowed in this house!"

Father forgot about his leg and lunged towards the door, where Bobcat was waiting to be let out.

The cat was too fast for him. He leapt up to the table and tried to jump up to the top beam the way he used to. But his lame leg fell out behind him, and his jump was broken. He flipped over onto Kate's bed and quickly sat upright, twitching his tail back and forth and glaring at Kate's father. A low growl rose in the cat's throat.

Kate flew over and stood in front of Bobcat. "This cat saved our lives," she stormed. Father glowered, but Kate didn't care. "How do you think we managed? There wasn't nearly enough food. We were down to nothing but sugar water when Bobcat started hunting for us. For two whole weeks he brought us a rabbit every day — and he would have kept going if he hadn't got hurt!"

Father's face went deadly white and he limped back to his chair. Kate knew he was in pain, but she wasn't finished. Quickly she shooed Bobcat outside. She stood by Father and glared at him, her hands on her hips, face flushed and eyes snapping.

"Bobcat is part of this family now, and we love him. If he leaves, well, well —" Kate searched for a suitable threat, "I'm leaving, too!"

Father's face went beet-red. "And just where do you think you'd go? Who would have you?"

"I could go home with Grandma Shaw. I know she'd take me."

"And the Shaws would ship you back fast enough!"

"Then I could go with Gajijáwi!"

"And live with the Mohawks? Don't be crazy, girl!"

"Gajijáwi has friends in King's Town. They'd find me a place."

"Doing what? You're a child!"

Kate stared at Father in disbelief. The injustice of it burnt in her throat. "Oh, really? You didn't seem to think so when you left me alone with the boys!"

Father opened his mouth to speak, then closed it again. Without saying another word, he limped over and fell into his bed with a low groan.

Kate put her sewing things and the special shawl back in the trunk. She slowly undressed and put on her nightgown.

As she pulled back the sheets and quietly crawled into bed beside Grandma Shaw, the old lady's hand came

up and patted Kate on the shoulder. She whispered,
"That a girl, Kate. Stand up for yourself."

CHAPTER
TWENTY-ONE

Grandma Shaw had breakfast ready when Kate and the boys opened their eyes. Kate woke up to the wonderful aroma and almost bounced out of bed like her brothers. Then a heavy feeling seemed to envelop her as she thought about her explosion at Father last night. She wasn't sorry for what she had said, but she didn't like this guilty feeling she had.

She wearily pulled on her clothes. She would have to face him sometime, she supposed. She hoped there wouldn't be another explosion — right in front of Grandma Shaw and Gajijáwi. She was glad that Father didn't know that Grandma Shaw had woken up last night when they had been shouting at each other.

Kate knew that in the eyes of the law and everyone else, her father was the boss. But it didn't seem fair. When it came to work and taking care of her brothers, Father expected her to act like a grown woman — and work like one.

"Kate, can you do up my breeches?" Ryan was nudging her. Kate automatically helped the boys fasten their clothes and finished dressing herself. When they slid along the bench for breakfast, Father was not at the head of the table. She looked across the cabin and saw that Father's quilt completely covered his head. He must still be asleep, she thought. She gave a sigh of relief. She would enjoy this breakfast, after all.

"This porridge is good!" said Alex.

Kate smiled. The hungry spell had sure changed the twins' attitude to food. Everything — even the porridge they used to complain about — was now wonderful. "Yes, it is good," Kate said. She decided she would just stop caring about Father's black moods. She was stuck with him until she was twenty-one or married, so she might as well learn to enjoy each day as it came — starting today.

This was washing day, she suddenly remembered. Where would they get the water? The snow water wasn't so clean now that the snow was melting and mixing with mud. She couldn't see how she'd get water from Hay Bay as they had last fall. There was not a good road for sled or wagon. Well, she would think about that after breakfast. She took another spoonful of her delicious oatmeal porridge.

A gentle tap came at the front door. Kate stepped lightly across the floor and swung the door open to let in Gajijáwi. To her surprise, Tówi was rolling a huge barrel up beside their stoop. She could see his panting sled dogs behind him. "From Hay Bay, this morning," Gajijáwi said.

"Thank you," Kate said. "I was wondering how we'd

manage." Their sled runners looked a little muddy, but the water looked clean and fresh.

Tówi hesitated on the doorstep. "Won't you come in and join us for breakfast?" Kate asked.

"I have eaten. Gajijáwi says you will have a busy day. I could take the boys to the sugar bush."

"Yes, let's go!" yelled Alex and Ryan. They had finished their breakfast, so Kate dressed them quickly in the their outer clothes and they were off.

Gajijáwi was joining Grandma Shaw for a cup of tea when they heard rustling from Father's bed. He emerged in a rumpled state; Kate guessed he had slept in his clothes.

"Good morning," said Grandma Shaw and Gajijáwi in lively tones.

Kate was amazed at how pleasant they sounded after Father's rude treatment of them the day before. Following their example, she said "Good morning" as cheerfully as she could. But she didn't look his way.

Father went over to the table, and Grandma Shaw served a cup of tea. "Thank you," he said and took a few sips. "This is good tea."

They all continued their meal in silence.

"Where are the boys?" Father asked a few minutes later.

"They've gone with Tówi to the sugar bush," said Gajijáwi. "They seem to love trying to help."

"They love the maple sugar even more," said Father. "It's a corker how they go for it."

"Tówi won't let them make themselves sick," said Gajijáwi.

"It's good of him to be bothered with them. They do become quite a handful cooped up inside. I don't know how you handled them snowed in here all winter, Kate."

Kate could hardly believe her ears. Father had actually complimented her. She stared at him as though she had not fully understood what he had said.

"Yes, Kate is a great amazement to all of us," said Grandma Shaw. "When we heard how she survived with the help of Bobcat, we could hardly believe it. God works in wondrous ways. But I say it was too much for any twelve year old. Even some adults did not survive this winter."

"I almost didn't," said Father. Then he became thoughtful and silent again.

When they had finished eating, Grandma Shaw said, "Now, Kate, after we finish the dishes, pull off all the bedding and collect the soiled clothes. It looks like it will be a sunny day, so we'll do a big wash."

Kate hurried. She wanted to enjoy every moment she had left with Grandma Shaw and Gajijáwi.

After the women had finished the dishes, they started to prepare for the big wash day. Gajijáwi began to heat water in kettles. Over the fire, one kettle would hold white clothes that would boil until they were clean. Grandma Shaw began to vigorously rub soft soap on all the stains on the coloured clothes.

Father whittled on his canes all morning. By noon, the little cabin was full of steam. Father finally managed to lean on his canes, grab his cloak, and hop out the door without touching his foot to the floor.

Kate followed him outside. He was standing on one leg on the cold stoop. "Would you like me to bring you out a chair?" she asked.

"Thank you, Kate. I would appreciate that," he said.

She took out one of the smaller chairs and Father sank into it. "Put on your coat, Kate," he said. "Maybe we could talk out here for a few minutes."

Kate slipped inside for her coat. She didn't see Grandma Shaw wink at Gajijáwi or the returning smile. She was only thinking about how her father actually wanted to talk to her, and for once he didn't sound angry.

"I didn't get much sleep last night," her father began. "I was thinking about you, Kate, and all your hard work, and how you saved the boys. You're really a fine daughter. And you may wear your mother's shawl anytime you want. It looked — fine on you. Just like it did on her."

Kate looked away from him to the tree line beyond their house and held her breath. Was Father actually going to talk about Mother at last?

Father opened his mouth to speak, then closed it again without saying a word. Suddenly he threw back his head and burst out laughing.

Kate was shocked. She couldn't remember when she had last heard her father laugh.

Grinning at her, he said, "Why, Kate, I never saw it before, but you are just like your mother. I do believe I have a grown woman on my hands now."

Kate sat down abruptly on the stoop. Her knees were shaking. "What do you mean, just like Mother?" she asked.

Father stared out to the trees, but spoke with a smile

in his voice. "Once, when you were about six, a famous singer came to Albany. Your mother took you to hear him, against my wishes. I thought you were too young."

"I remember," said Kate.

Father looked up. "I'm not surprised," he nodded. "Your mother said you would."

"It was beautiful. Everyone was dressed up, and the music was so thrilling. Mother kept squeezing my hand so hard it hurt. She'd apologize and then do it again. No one wanted to leave, and it got really late — way past dinnertime. We sure left a trail of dust behind us all the way home."

Father laughed. "When you finally arrived, I was pretty hungry and even more angry with your mother than when you'd left! Well, your mother just handed you the reins and hopped down from the buggy. She marched right up to me, hands on her hips —" Father smiled at Kate "— the way yours were last evening — and invited me inside."

"I always wondered what she said," Kate said shyly. "You came out a few minutes later, and you were so kind and gentle, and you let me help you feed and brush the horses."

"Why, she just spoke her mind, that's all. She told me it was a once-in-a-lifetime opportunity and that you'd remember it all your life, and what was a late supper compared to that? And she was right," said Father. He was silent for a while, then shook his head and chuckled. "Only you remember a lot more than even *she* counted on!"

Father reached over and took Kate's hand.

"I know I — I've been hard on you sometimes, Kate," he said awkwardly. "And I'm sorry about that. But when your mother died . . . we were so disappointed when our other babies died, you see, and then when she carried the boys full term, we hardly dared hope . . ." Father fell silent for a moment. His face was full of pain. He went on, "I don't know what I'm trying to say, really. Except, if your mother was here, she'd be right proud of you, Kate."

Kate didn't know where to look or what to say. It was the first time since Mother died that Father had spoken of her with joy. Her heart felt like it was bursting.

Just then Bobcat came crawling up the steps with his back leg dragging. He rubbed against Kate's leg. Kate reached out her hand and stroked him.

"Better let him inside," said Father. "He's one of the family now."

CHAPTER
TWENTY-TWO

"And that's how we survived the winter, Sarah!" Kate was sitting with her friend in the fern glade, patting Bobcat on the back. Robins and song sparrows were singing in nearby trees, keeping well out of the cat's range.

"Bobcat, you are a wonder!" said Sarah.

It was the third week of May, and the Shaws and two other families from Adolphustown had come up to help Father build a proper home. Of the Shaw children only Sarah and Albert had come. Their mother had stayed home to care for the younger ones. They would be taking Grandma Shaw back home with them. Gajijáwi had left a month ago when the maple syrup run had ended.

The girls could hear axes ringing against the pines on the other side of the cabin. "Listen to those axes!" Kate smiled. "What a great sound! With its movable corner-posts, the sooner that old cabin becomes a storage shed the better!"

"But I loved that part, Kate! It would be marvelous to sleep in a cabin that moved . . . just like an old ship. How exciting!"

"Yes, you could say it was exciting — especially when the curtains caught fire."

"The curtains caught fire?" Sarah gasped.

"Yes, from the candle I'd put in front of the window."

"That's one way to warm up the cabin, I suppose!" Sarah stifled a giggle at her own joke.

"Sarah, it was serious," Kate frowned. "We could have died." Then her frown turned into a smile. It was impossible to be anything but happy today. "I guess it does seem kind of funny, looking back," she admitted. "But I sure wasn't laughing when that big tree limb fell down on the cabin and caved in part of our roof."

"I know! That must have been awful, just awful!"

Kate stood up and brushed off the back of her skirt. "I want to forget about it! Now let's go back and see if it's time to eat." Sarah stood up, too, and they chatted as they walked along.

When they reached the clearing, Kate saw that the women had been busy. They had brought the table outside and set up benches and chairs around it.

"Watch this!" said Alex, running to Kate. He threw a stick towards the forest and the Shaws' dog, Rover, raced across the clearing after it. "Isn't he the greatest?" Alex grinned.

"No, Bobcat's the greatest!" Ryan said. Just then Bobcat gave a loud meow from the roof of the old cabin.

Kate pointed to Bobcat and smiled at Sarah.

Rover pelted over to the cabin and started barking at the cat.

"C'mon, Rover! Mind your manners," said Albert,

who had come up behind the boys.

"Dinnertime!" called Grandma Shaw. "Sarah, you come and help me bring out the food. Kate, you round up your brothers." She was as jolly as ever. She and the other women were carrying basswood bowls and spoons and setting them out on the table.

"Come to the table," Kate said to the boys, who were beside Albert, patting his dog.

"I wish we could keep him." Alex looked up at Albert with pleading eyes.

"I'm afraid not," Albert said. "Rover and I got really attached this winter. But if Rover fathers pups, I'll bring you one."

"Oh, boy! I'd love that!" Alex turned to Ryan. "Wouldn't that be great?"

"Yes, but . . ." Ryan looked worried.

"Oh, I'm sure he'll like cats all right," said Albert. "I bet he'll be getting along fine with Bobcat in no time at all."

Kate smiled at Albert. He had managed to make both of the twins happy — not always the easiest task, she knew. He was a very nice boy, she thought, and hand-some, too.

Then to her surprise, Albert said, "Now I'll have an excuse to come back and visit you again."

Had she heard correctly? Had he said, "visit you again"?

Uncertain, she answered, "I'd like that — to have you and Sarah visiting. It was awful lonely last winter."

"Oh, sure, I'll bring Sarah," Albert said. "But I might

have to come by myself sometimes, just to get a word in edgewise." He rumpled Alex's hair, but the look he gave Kate held a question. Kate's cheeks, already glowing in the bright sunlight, flushed even more. A strange new happiness filled her, and she lowered her eyes. She would think about this later.

"Come to the table, now, everyone," Grandma Shaw announced.

Kate found Sarah and sat beside her. The twins sat on Kate's other side. Rover went over to the table, too, and sat down right behind Albert and the twins. When they were all at their places, they bowed their heads and Father gave thanks. "For good friends and our health this day, we thank you. And for this food, too, we are especially grateful. We ask for guidance and help for all of us in the year ahead. Amen."

"You forgot Bobcat," Ryan said loudly. "You forgot to thank God for Bobcat."

"I believe I did forget," Father said. "You may do that, Ryan."

They all bowed their heads again. In a much quieter voice, Ryan began, "Thank you for Bobcat. Thank you for all the rabbits he brought us. And thank you for healing his leg so that he can play with us and climb trees again."

Alex gave Ryan a sharp jab in the ribs.

"Ouch!" yelled Ryan. "He . . ."

"Amen," said Father, smiling. "Now, let's eat." Grandma Shaw brought out the iron pot full of beaver, pigeon, and corn stew. From his end of the table Father ladled the food into everyone's bowls.

"Brought you some seed, David," Mr. Shaw said with his mouth full of stew.

"Will, don't talk with your . . ." Grandma Shaw began, but she stopped herself in mid-sentence and smiled. "Oh, well, I'm grateful we have food again."

"Look!" said Father, rising from the bench. "It's our Mohawk friends from Tyendinaga. Kate, go fetch some more bowls."

As they drew near, Father stepped over to greet them.

"We're just passing through," said Desagósnye. He handed Father two freshly killed rabbits.

"That'll make a delicious supper," said Grandma Shaw, as Father came over to her with the fresh meat. She took it and hurried into the cabin.

"Please join us at the table," Father said. "You've come at just the right time to meet my friends to the south." Turning to the others, he said, "Desagósnye and Tówi saved my life, and Gajijáwi cared for my children."

"Gajijáwi!" Kate exclaimed. "Come and sit between me and Sarah. Remember how I told you about Sarah?" Gajijáwi smiled and came over to meet Kate's friend.

Grandma Shaw hurried out of the cabin with a pot full of boiled frogs and wild rice. She had been saving it for supper, but now they would share it with their friends. And she'd have time to prepare a scrumptious rabbit stew for the evening meal.

Bright rays of sunlight filled the O'Carrs' clearing and glinted across the table. Kate took a deep breath, filling her lungs with spring air and her nose with the smells of good food and freshly cut wood. She looked at her Father, and he smiled warmly at her.

Happily, Kate dipped her spoon into her stew and ate.

HISTORICAL NOTE

Historical accounts of Loyalists tell about the notorious Hungry Year. In the Bay of Quinte area and the Upper St. Lawrence, it began in the winter of 1787 and continued until the harvest of 1788.

In 1787, the meagre handouts from the British government stopped. That same year, the growing season was crippled by severe drought and followed by an extremely cold and long winter. Bays and rivers were covered with two feet of ice, so fishing was not possible. Snowdrifts were so deep that wild animals were unable to find forage; even hunting was poor.

In *History of the Settlement of Upper Canada*, William Canniff, one of the oldest historians of the Loyalist experience, gives evidence of the harshness of the winter of 1788. He quotes Henry Ruttan, an old-timer and an ex-sheriff.

The snow was unusually deep, so that the deer became an easy prey to their rapacious enemies, the wolves, who fattened on their destruction, whilst men were perishing for want. Five individuals, in different places [in Fredericksburgh], were found dead, and one poor woman also, with a live infant at her breast (p. 199).

The events in this book are taken from true stories of the Hungry Year, collected by historians. In Leslie Hannon's *Redcoats and Loyalists*, Bobcat's story is summed up in these words:

A desperate father left his family in the winter bush to search for food. When he got back eight days later with some supplies, he found wife and children in fine shape. During his absence, the family tabby cat, which had never before shown the slightest enterprise, appeared every day with a rabbit (p. 54).

Although my central family is fictional, I have borrowed their names from real people. The Loyalist name O'Carr comes from my own family tree; the O'Carrs had Irish roots and immigrated to Canada from the State of Maine in 1783. Daniel Carr, a volunteer in the Loyal Rangers, received five hundred acres for his service and settled on a portion of this land in Earnesttown, which bordered the east side of Fredericksburgh.

Other characters and places in the story are not fictional. John W. Meyers is an historical figure who appears in my books *Flight* and *Meyers' Creek*. Adolphustown was originally named Hollandville after Surveyor-General Major Samuel Holland, but kept that name for only a short period. Because the hamlet had access to water transportation, it thrived. Frank B. Edwards writes in *The Smiling Wilderness* that the hamlet and the township led Ontario in the establishment of many institutions, including "courts, municipal government, and the Methodist Church" (p. 81). Adolphustown's fortunes sank with the arrival of the railway through Napanee in the 1850s, however. Today, Adolphustown is the site of a provincial park, a cultural centre, and a museum.

It took many years for settlements to develop, and the first Loyalists lived in primitive, often isolated dwellings. In *The Smiling Wilderness*, Frank B. Edwards tells of living trees used as cornerposts for some early shanties. The swaying is also recorded in older sources.

Tyendinaga Township was the actual home of Loyalist Mohawks, as described in the story. The Mohawks under Joseph Brant had fought for the British in the Revolutionary War. This large group settled with Brant around the present-day Brantford area. Some of the Mohawks left the group under their chief Captain John Deserontyou and settled in the Bay of Quinte area in 1784 (*Places of Ontario: Their Name Origins and History*, p. 545). In 1793, the entire two-thousand acre township was deeded to them by Lieutenant Governor John Graves Simcoe as a reward for their loyalty to the British Crown. In 1835, John Culbertson, a grandson of Captain Deserontyou, applied to the Mohawk chiefs for a parcel of land at the eastern end of the reserve. Eventually, he had a village plot surveyed there and named it Deseronto in honour of his grandfather (ibid., p. 545-46).

The Mohawk characters in my story are fictional, but the assistance they offered the O'Carrs is based on fact. Many Loyalists were saved from perishing by the friendly help of native people, both Mohawks from Tyendinaga and Missisaugas (from whom the British had bought the land). They were more knowledgeable about the countryside and knew which herbs were safe to eat. They passed on this knowledge to the early white settlers and taught them to harvest wild rice and plant corn.

Native people also taught the Loyalists how to make garments out of deerskin and shared with them the secret of how to make maple syrup, "their greatest gesture of friendship" (Bev McKay, *Sugar Bush*, p. 11). By teaching the Loyalists these things, as well as the arts of canoeing, snowshoeing, and using herbs as medicines, the native people showed great generosity.

At that time in history, the role of women was very different among the Mohawks than it was among the white population. They took an active role in planning for the tribe and had a voice in council meetings and battle planning. The fact that they controlled the Mohawks' food supply gave them real clout. On the other hand, white men had complete control over white women. Gradually in Canada, as the white man's law took over, native women began to lose their power too. It took over a century, until the time when Nellie L. McClung helped to change the status of all women in Canada, for women to win some control over their own lives.

The Loyalist families who came to Upper Canada

endured severe and life-threatening hardships. They suffered terribly and some died during the worst period of the postwar time — The Hungry Year. But they did not lose hope in their new country, Canada, nor faith in God. With determination, endurance, and great courage, they kept struggling on until life became better.